Sam
and the
Pixie:

Finding Faith

Sabine Chennault

Dear Taylor,
always believe in your dreams and follow your heart!
Sabine ☺

PALOMA BOOKS   ASHLAND, OREGON

SAM AND THE PIXIE: FINDING FAITH
©2020 SABINE CHENNAULT
Published by Paloma Books
(An imprint of L&R Publishing, LLC)

All rights reserved. No part of this publication may be reproduced or used in any form or by any means, graphic, electronic or mechanical, including photocopying, recording, taping, or information and retrieval systems without written permission of the publisher. This is a work of fiction. Names, characters, businesses, places, events and incidents are either the products of the author's imagination or used in a fictitious manner. Any resemblance to actual persons, living or dead, or actual events is purely coincidental.

Paloma Books
PO Box 3531
Ashland, OR 97520
www.palomabooks.com

Interior design: Sasha Kincaid
Cover design: L. Redding
Cover art (front): Tansie Stephens

Cataloging-in-Publication Data is available from the publisher on request.
ISBN: 978-1-55571-981-4

Printed and bound in the United States of America
First edition 10 9 8 7 6 5 4 3 2

Dedications

For my better half and loving husband, Lance D.
Chennault. My biggest fan and best critic. Thank you
for your selfless twenty years of service in the Navy,
and all of your help, love, and support.

Special thanks to my parents, Helene and Peter Jury,
for always believing in me; my children, Samantha,
Jesse, and Jennifer; and my grandchildren, Julianna and
Nick, who have kept me inspired through their years of
growing with mostly vivid imaginations.

A heartfelt "thank you" goes to Tansie Stephens
and her great talent for photo manipulation; my
wonderful partner, Lance, for his photography
expertise; and my daughter, Samantha, for graciously
standing in as her namesake "Sam" for the cover.

IV   SAM AND THE PIXIE: FINDING FAITH

Prologue

The children scattered across the large yard in all directions. Some stopped here and there trying to find the perfect hiding place, others concentrated so deeply that a popping balloon made them jump. When they realized what had happened they all giggled.

The popping balloon caused Maggie to drop a tray of cookies and Alvin jumped out of his chair. Sam stood at the bottom of the patio steps and looked as if she was in deep thought. She didn't seem to have even heard the pop.

"What on earth…?" Maggie looked at her husband. As the two of them realized what had happened they began to laugh. The kids had already forgotten about the incident. Some of them were still looking for just the right place to hide.

"Lizzy, you don't seem to like the fact that you got stuck counting?" Alvin asked the eight-year-old-girl sitting on the steps. "It's not that Mr. G," she smiled, "there are a lot of kids and twice as many really cool hiding places." She turned away from him, buried her face in her hands and continued counting from where she had left off.

Alvin and Maggie couldn't help but smile at each other.

"Do you need any help bringing out the goodies?" Alvin asked his wife. "Yes dear, that would be nice." She smiled at him. "Let me just fire up the grill really quick," he headed towards the corner of the house.

"I think Rob is already working on that," Maggie interrupted him. The two of them headed into the house through the white double doors and left it open.

The long wooden table on the patio had been covered in a bright yellow tablecloth. Daisy-patterned plates, cups, and napkins were placed on the table to serve twelve little girls. The other guests would be sitting at tables, which had been placed in the yard but matched in table coverings.

All the kids had found hiding places but Sam had a special place, a spot not just good for hiding today, but all sorts of other things. This had been her special place for as long

as she could remember. She snuck around the side of the old farmhouse, opposite from where her older brother Rob has just started the grill. She followed the narrow path, which lead to the garden gate. To each side of the gate was a beautiful hedge and the gate itself was covered by an arch. It had a vine of bush roses growing all over it and the smell was wonderful. Right next to the gate sat an old metal tub, which grandma used to collect water for the small plants in her small greenhouse. When there was no water in it, Sam would use it as a place to hide or just sit and look at a picture book.

She didn't care about dirtying her pretty yellow sundress, she climbed into the tub and ducked down enough to not be seen from the path. From her crouched position the smell of the roses was powerful.Even though the tub was a bit uncomfortable, she couldn't help but love it. Actually, she loved the whole farm, it was so much fun to play with the lambs and the small bunnies. Her mom had told her that this was the last year that she would be able to have her party at grandma's farm since she was now old enough to go to school. Dad had told her that if she wanted to have her parties at the farm, it would have to be on weekends. That didn't help much, but it did make it a little easier. Didn't they realize that if she had less time to spend at the farm her chances of finding a Pixie would decrease? Why didn't grown-upsunderstand these things?

"Hey squirt," Rob looked down at his little sister, "You're gonna get your dress all dirty in there."

"Rob, please go away, you'llgive away my hiding place," Sam stated rather loudly, "and besides my dress won't get that dirty. There is always water in here, so it's clean." She crossed her arms on her chest as if to tell him that she wasn't happy with his standing there. *Older brothers, jeez, they are almost as bad as parents.*

"Ok, just came to tell let you know that most of the other kids are back on the patio. I think there are only a couple others besides you that haven't been found," he smiled at her.

"I bet that's Jen and Jules, I showed them the coolest spot by the edge of the forest, remember the one you showed me?" Sam asked proudly. Rob laughed and nodded, "Ok squirt, see you back on the patio for cake, ice cream, and burgers." With that, he walked back to the house, Sam heard him giggle for most of the way. For some reason he did that a lot. She often would say something that made him giggle. Rob was just four years older than her. Jules and Jen were the only ones who seemed to share her great interest in Pixies and Faeries. They had spent a lot of time together at the farm and most of it had been spent exploring the huge garden, yard, and the edge of the forest for anything that sparkled. She was sure that Pixies sparkled because of how beautiful they were. Rob had tricked them lots of times.

No sooner had she finished her thought when something resembling a speck of dust fell down right in front of her eyes. She thought it was odd, and must be pollen. Grandma had explained all that stuff to her last year when she had wanted to know why there were so many bees in the flower garden. Another speck of dust, and this time it glistened in the sunlight. It sparkled really super, shiny, colorful glitter. It landed on her dress, and as she fluffed it, the dust sparkled again. She stood up, wondering where was it coming from, she no longer cared if anyone saw her… this had to be investigated. Still standing in the tub, she looked up at the roses. She had to guard her eyes from the sun with one hand so she could see better. There it was again…amazing! Just where could it be coming from and more importantly, what was causing it?

She inspected each rose within her reach while standing in the tub before getting out to check the other side. She started at the bottom of the garden arch and looked inside each and every single flower. Nothing, she went back to the tub, got in it and waited. There it was again, it came from one of the flowers she apparently had missed earlier. It wasn't high at all and she must have passed it when she stood up.

Sparkling dust sprinkled out of one open rose as Sam carefully leaned over and looked inside.

Could it be possible? No, there was just no way. Her mouth and eyes were wide open and she forgot to breathe. There it was, right in the middle of the flower – a Pixie, struggling to get loose from something. Sam couldn't move and it seemed like minutes before she was able to take a breath.

She wanted to yell for Jen and Jules, but she realized that it would scare the little creature and it may cause her to fly away. Her wings were extended as far as they could go and she had not yet noticed Sam. She, on the other hand, was sure that the Pixie was a girl because she had long red hair, so did Sam. Her wings were beautiful and light green, and Sam could see right through them. She so wanted to reach into the flower and help the little creature but she knew she couldn't. Mom and grandma had read her countless stories about Pixies and Faeries and she knew all their rules. What was she to do? There was no way she could get the attention of her two friends to help her with this.

"Sam…Sam!!!!" Sue, her much older sister, came around the corner of the house yelling for her. Sue was already fifteen and made fun of Sam all the time for believing in them. She also didn't like that Mom and Dad encouraged Sam to believe in whatever she wanted. Sam couldn't understand why that bothered her so much, they did the same with her, but she must not think about that. Luckily, Sue stopped a few feet away, "Hey squirt, don't you hear me calling you?" Sue asked, obviously annoyed.

Sam nodded, "What do you want?" she asked her sister and quickly glanced back to see if the Pixie had moved. Apparently the little creature had not paid attention to the noise as she was too busy trying to free herself.

"I don't want anything, brat, but your guests would like you to come eat with them." Now Sue was really upset. Sam shook her head and turned her attention back to the Pixie, who seemed to have run out of energy. She sat in the flower with her elbows on her knees and her head lying on one hand. Her foot seemed to still be stuck. Sam realized she couldn't stay and figured she would just come back after cake and ice cream. She climbed out of the tub and ran past her sister to the patio. All of her guests, her brother, Mom, Dad, and grandma were already seated at two tables. Everyone had a plate with either a hot dog or hamburger in front of them. Sam quickly settled on a hot dog thinking she would be able to eat that faster. Just a few bites and she could go, a hamburger would take at least twice as long, if not more. She wondered if she could get the attention of Jen and Jules for a few minutes. It didn't seem possible.

With her mouth still full, she asked if they could now have cake and ice cream.

"Good grief little girl," Maggie shook her head, "where is the fire?"

"Nowhere, Mom," Sam attempted to say with a mouth full of hot dog, "Just need to go check on something."

Alvin went inside to get the ice cream and Maggie got the cake from a little table sitting of to the side of the patio. She placed six little pink candles in a beautiful pink cake covered with little flowers and placed it in front of Sam. Alvin lit the candles and the whole group began to sing "Happy Birthday." Before they were done, Sam had blown out the candles and bugged her mom to start cutting the cake.

"Honey I am a little concerned with your rush," Maggie seemed a little irritated, "Aren't you enjoying your party?"

"I am mom, I really am," Sam smiled holding a fork full of cake in front of her mouth. "I just saw something really cool right before Sue came and got me and I want to see if it's still there so I can share it with Jen and Jules."

"Honey I am sure it will still be there after a while, just wait till things settle down a bit. I'm sure whatever it is will still be there later," Maggie rubbed Sam's head. "I'm not," whispered Sam. As if all of this wasn't taking long enough, now they all wanted her to open her gifts. She agreed reluctantly and insisted that Jen and Jules sat next to her, maybe she could get a chance to tell them what she saw in between gifts.

She grabbed Jen's arm as soon as she sat down, "You will not believe what happened…that is so awesome Rob, thank you…I was in the tub… you know the one by the gate?"

She tried to talk to her friends and thank her brother for his gift at the same time. The only thing that made her lose focus for a few minutes was the gift from her parents, an Easy Bake Oven she had wanted for a long time. Finally, she would be able to bake things on her own. but that wasn't important right now. She managed to work her way through the gifts and the moment she had opened the last one and thanked the person she had gotten it from, the three girls hopped out of their seats.

The three of them stopped a few feet away from the tub. Sam continued on her own,climbed into the tub and reached for the rose. Her hand was shaking as she gently pulled the flower towards her. She looked inside. The Pixie was gone. Sam slowly let go of the flower and looked at her friends. Jules held her hand in front of her mouth and Jen just stood there.

Sam shook her head to let them know that the little creature was no longer there. She slowly sat down in the tub as her friends ran over to her. Jules climbed in the tub and squeezed down in front of Sam wrapping her arms around her friend. Jen leaned over the side and hugged her as well. Sam couldn't help but cry and it took the girls several minutes to calm her down. They told her that if she truly believed it in her heart she would see another one someday.

Several minutes past before Sam and Jules climbed out of the tub and three friends headed back to the house. Half way between the tub and the house Jen stopped and told the girls to wait a second. She ran back to the tub, climbed into it and reached for the rose that had contained the Pixie just a little while ago. She broke off the flower, stuck her nose into it to smell it and ran back to her friends.

"You can put this in the book Jules and I gave you, it will be a nice memory," Jen said as she handed Sam the flower. Sam looked into it and saw it still contained some of the dust that had sparkled so magically.

"She hugged Jen, "This is the best gift I have ever gotten."

Back at the patio she carefully placed the rose in the book about Pixies Jen and Jules had given her as a gift, it remains there to this day.

⇒ 1 ⇐

Beginning or End?

Mariskina sat quietly in a corner while Faith's dad paced slowly back and forth. His face had grown bright red with anger, and he hadn't uttered a single word in over five minutes. Faith stood silently in the middle of the room, afraid to move so much as the smallest muscle.

Five minutes ago, her dad had started a sentence, and she was very afraid of how he would finish it.

"The only way you will understand the severity of what you have done is if I …well…if I—" Not a word since then. He had given her a few angry glares, but nothing more.

"Maliek," Mariskina spoke his name very gently as if not to interrupt his train of thought, "maybe you could find a way to overlook this. Nothing happened. She wasn't even seen by anyone." She stopped and looked at Faith. "Were you?" she asked.

"No, Wise One," replied Faith, swallowing hard in order to hold back the tears. Her dad stopped and gave Mariskina a look that Faith was sure could have knocked her wings off.

Faith knew that Mariskina had read her father's mind. It must be something awful or she would not have interrupted him. Before another thought could cross her mind, she heard her father shout, "You always protect these young ones. In your heart they cannot do anything wrong. What will happen in this community if these young ones do not learn the ways of the past?"

The room grew darker as the sun began to set. Faith had lost all concept of how long she had been standing there but knew she didn't want to hear what was coming. Her dad had never taken this long to come up with the proper punishment.

"D-Daddy?" Faith's voice was shaking. She was still trying to hold back the tears. His head now swung around, and she looked into a face she had never seen before.

"You will be silent," he yelled, "until I have made a decision!" He walked to the window and watched the sunlight turn everything it touched into a golden shimmer. "Faith, I am sorry to say this, but I see no other alternative." He turned away from the window and started pacing again. He only crossed the floor twice before he stopped in front of Faith. "You treat the safety of our community as if it is nothing."

Mariskina stepped toward him, "No Maliek, think of the consequences."

"Silence, Old One, your comments are not wanted," Maliek answered gruffly, turning his attention back to his daughter. "So, my dear child, I am well aware of the consequences and what you may face, but there will be no lighting ceremony tomorrow." He spoke gently, as if all of the anger had vanished.

As he took her face in his hand, Faith could feel the warmth of her tears streaming down her face. She had never seen this coming. "No, Dad," she said, her voice quivering as she spoke. He turned away from her and walked back to the window.

"Maliek," Mariskina broke in, "you can't do that. If it doesn't happen tomorrow, it can't ever happen. This is unheard of," she insisted. "No Pixie has ever been banned from the lighting ceremony. She faces banishment from the tree!"

"No Pixie has ever disregarded the safety of her home the way Faith has. That is also unheard of," replied Maliek. While the two of them glared at each other the door suddenly slammed against the wall. Faith was gone.

Though Mariskina was much smaller than Maliek, her powerful presence made her seem taller. "I know you are her father and have the highest in rank in the tree, but here I must step in. I will call an emergency meeting of the Tree Council. You will destroy her life if you prevent her from attending the lighting ceremony. You know very well that her wings will become useless."

She paused to see if he would say anything, but he remained silent. Her glare of anger now turned to fear. His royal blue knickers and coat made him look older than the 120 years he had counted for himself. All the hair from his head had migrated to his chin.

There were now only thirteen of the original Windhill Tree Pixies left that made up the Council of Elders. Mariskina was ninety-three years older than Maliek, but since she had left Windhill Tree for almost sixty years, she was not allowed to act as the head of the Council. If she had been permitted leadership, this would never have happened. Oh sure, there would have been punishment, but not until after the ceremony.

"I demand, as your elder, that you reconsider your decision," she insisted. "If you won't, then we need to let the council decide. You cannot make that kind of decision without the council, not even for your own child." Not waiting for a reply, Mariskina left Maliek standing by the window.

Faith sat on top of the same red-capped mushroom she always came to when she needed to pout or just think. This time it was for an unusually long time. The sun had just begun to shine through the canopy of the trees, causing Faith's translucent green wings to shimmer in the beaming light. Both the creases that ran between her almond-shaped, dark-green eyes and the twitch she got in one of her pointed ears gave away the state of deep thought in which she had fallen.

Faith didn't feel she was like other Windhill Tree Pixies, she never had. Instead, she had always thought that she had more distinct human features, like the freckles that were scattered across her nose and under her eyes. The other girls in the tree had shimmering, golden hair, but Faith's hair was red as the mushroom she sat on, and her wings were also a deeper green. Her mother always told her that it was because she simply had a much-deeper connection to the forest. Faith didn't care.

She was now a day away from her seventeenth birthday, and her idiot brother Frizzle had told their father that she had been going to the clearing almost every day.

She knew very well that the clearing was off limits to all of the Windhill Tree Pixies. In fact, she had been told not to go there at least a few hundred times since she was nine, and she had always known that the punishment for taking such a risk would be severe. Someday it would catch up to her. Yet, never in a million sprinkles of Pixie dust had she expected to hear what her father had said.

Suddenly, she noticed a movement in the clearing. There were young people—human people—the same people she had been watching in fascination for several days.

She thought they were probably about her age, they always looked like they had a lot of fun, and one of the girls looked like Faith. She had bright red hair that hung just past her chin, and it looked totally unruly. The other humans called her Sam. She had freckles all over the place, and she was a bit shorter than the others. Faith was curious about this one they called Sam, and that was the reason she had decided to come back to the clearing as much as she did. So now again, she sat on her mushroom, thinking and watching.

Even though Sam was smaller than the others, she ran as fast as the boys and could climb a tree just as swiftly and easily. She seemed like someone Faith would like to be friends with. Well, at least she would like to know more about her.

Faith's dad had never been so mad at her. In her mind, he simply wasn't capable of doing that, it was just unheard of. It wasn't just the day of the lighting celebration, but it was also her birthday.

The lighting ceremony was held for all Pixies when they turned seventeen. There was no other day for it. The changing Pixie is placed in the center of the tree, and all others fly through and around the tree and light it up. It's beautiful and is the most important day in a Pixie's life. Your wings don't light up until you turn seventeen, and only through the power of all the others are your own wings able to light. With that light came all the powers an adult Pixie possessed in her Pixie dust.

If her wings didn't get lit, she wouldn't get her powers, and her wings would turn dull and useless. After some time she wouldn't be able to fly anymore, and that was just the least of the problems.

How long had she been sitting on her mushroom? She now had just over twenty-hours left to change his mind.

But how?

What could she possibly do?

Is the ceremony to be held today? If so, she was running out of time.

Surely by now everyone in the tree must have thought that she had run away from home. Why hadn't anyone been here looking for her? Mariskina was the oldest Pixie in the tree, but no one was allowed to knock at her door before the sun was at its highest point. So, Faith had to wait awhile. If she didn't get her wings lit, she could be banned from the tree. There was no use for an adult Pixie whose wings didn't light up.

"Sam, get away from there. You know those mushrooms are poisonous," Faith heard someone yell.

She was startled out of her deep thought only to look up at a huge face with big green eyes looking right back at her. She nearly tumbled off the mushroom cap but managed to catch herself on a little hole the ants had eaten.

Sam just stood there, her mouth and eyes wide open, a total look of disbelief on her face. Faith tried to think what to do. Should she just fall off the cap into the high grass beneath her and keep still, or should she make a lot of noise to scare Sam away?

'Honestly as if that will work,' she thought to herself.

If only this had happened after the wing-lighting ceremony. She could have simply flown up, lit her wings, and Sam would never have remembered seeing her. But that wasn't an option. She was left with no other choice but to drop off the mushroom. She tried like crazy to remember how far down it was. Could she break something if she fell the wrong way?

She backed up ever so slightly, hoping that Sam would not be able to notice her movement. When she reached the edge of the cap, she turned her head to see how far down it was. "Wow," she said out loud.

The knots in her stomach tightened, and she closed her eyes at the same time she let herself fall backward. With a slight thump, not noticeable to a human ear, she landed on the ground ... well, so she thought anyway. She lay there for a moment, enjoying the warmth of the soft moss. Wait, it was still fairly early in the morning, so the moss wouldn't be warm. It would be cool and wet, as the sun had not had time to dry and warm it up just yet.

What had she landed on?

She slowly opened her eyes. She was sitting on this huge pink thing. It was warm and soft but uglier than a toad with a bad head cold.

There were five pieces sticking out from it. What were those things—branches? Was this some type of new tree? She had never in all her life seen anything like this. It seemed to be trembling as well. Flyspit! Could she be dead?

She poked at the pink thing, and it started to wiggle. "What is it, Sam?" A deep, loud voice called from behind. "Wow, what is it … a bug?" The words had come from a voice that sounded almost like her brother's. Then another voice barked, "You nimrod, bugs don't have bright red hair. Sam, are you OK?"

Faith felt as if she had been lifted up ever so slowly. Then, just as she was about to turn and face whatever was behind her, she felt this incredibly warm air cover her whole body—and it was horrible.

It smelled just like the medicine Mariskina once made her take when she got into blue scraggle. Why didn't she listen to her dad … oh, Fairy Lights, what were those things? Three huge faces were at once staring and breathing down on her. The horrible smell came from the mouth of one of them and whatever he was chewing.

Faith was so close to Sam's face that she could have counted the freckles on her face. The chewing face came closer.

"That thing doesn't look so good. Maybe being touched by a human will kill it—you know, how when you like touch a butterfly."

'Something has to be done', Faith thought, but just what, she didn't know. Touched by a human? What did smelly face mean? She hadn't touched a human—or had she? She looked at Sam's hand. It **was** what she was standing on!

She looked past all of them through a little gap between their heads. One of them had walked away and was now on his way back. She realized that they only looked small from a distance. She knew they were bigger than Pixies but she had no idea how much. She had never seen one so close. She realized that what she was standing on was the hand of a human, and not just any human, but a girl named Sam.

"Oh please holy branches of Butterfield greens. I promise I will not ever disobey my father again," Faith said out loud. "Please don't let them squash me, Mariskina ... please help me." Her teacher had told her many stories about Pixies who had gotten too close to humans and were later discovered smashed—or at least never seen again. With that thought, Faith felt her knees turn to mush, and then lights went out around her. She fainted.

≥ 2 ≤
The Council Decides

Maliek remained by the window. His heart had never felt so heavy. He wondered if he had he made the right decision? Well, he would let the Council decide. As long as he had been alone with the children he had always expected this kind of trouble out of Faith's younger brother, Frizzle, but not from her, not his Faith.

It was dark now, and he knew the news had spread throughout the tree. He stepped outside of the door, which had remained open since Faith had left. He went to a small porch just opposite the door and reached up to grab a golden, flower-shaped trumpet. Placing the trumpet to his lips, he blew it three times, hung it back up, then turned and spread his brightly lit, pale-green wings. Within seconds, he had reached the top of the tree, along with Mariskina and the other eleven Council members.

Nisse, the tallest of all the Pixies in Windhill Tree, patted Maliek on the back. "We've heard, sir. We need to decide quickly."

"Maliek," Mariskina interrupted, "I am sorry I was so harsh before, I hope you understand my concern. Has anyone started searching for her yet?"

He looked up at the stars that seemed to grow brighter as he watched them. "Yes, Old One," he said quietly, "several of the young ones are out looking for her. Frizzle knows of a special place she likes to visit, but he's not sure where it is."

Mariskina lowered her head with sadness. What was to happen? Of all 117 young ones in the tree, Faith was her favorite. She had always been. There was just something about her that set her apart from the others. She didn't have a hard time learning all of the names of flowers, and the multitude of medicinal purposes of all the herbs just seemed to come to her without any effort.

When the Pixies were children and she had sent small groups into the forest to collect particular herbs, Faith had always brought back the right ones. There were countless times she had to brew a batch of Heilkrauter, because one of the children had brought blue scraggle instead of blue pestile. The two herbs look almost identical.

As a smidgeling, a Pixie under ten years of age, Faith had looked just like all the others. With blond hair and pale-green wings, she was even a bit smaller than all the other new Pixies. It had just been in the last six years that her hair had, for some reason, gone to bright red. For the same odd and unknown reason, her wings had turned a deep green, and she had gotten freckles. Mariskina couldn't remember ever having met a Pixie with freckles.

Faith refused to leave the family hollow for days when the first freckles had shown up. Things got even worse for her once her wings started getting darker. Other Pixies, especially Frizzle, teased her. Mariskina and Maliek repeatedly warned him to stop teasing her, but nothing seemed to help.

The whole thing got so bad that the Council of Elders gathered to consider the matter. This was something completely unheard of. It was normal for Council gatherings to be called for mundane matters dealing with celebration deliberations—what needed to be done in case two of the young ones turned seventeen on the same day, or what food and drink selections needed to be made for certain occasions, but nothing like the changes of a youngling had ever been discussed.

At the Council meeting about the matter, it took every bit of strength Starline could muster to keep from bursting out laughing. Being one of the elders, she herself had twenty-six children in all, living in various trees throughout the country. She had more Pixie children than any of the other elders and had heard a lot of strange stories and worries. This was the sort of problem that could really come only from a child, even though this was the best she had ever heard. Even she didn't know why Faith was changing. It did explain a lot.

In the end no one knew what to do and it was Faith and Mariskina's friend Starline who made all the difference. So took Faith to visit her grandmother at nearby Oakwashtree. The two of them spent a lot of time discussing flowers, herbs, nature, and Faith's freckle situation. Apparently, Faith felt as if she had done something to upset nature, and she was now condemned to die. These very obvious changes were to let everyone else know that nature herself was punishing her.

Starline took several days to talk with Faith. When they returned to Windhill Tree, she felt she had succeeded. Starline's own second-youngest now believed that Faith's changes were indeed not a punishment but an honor from nature. Starline convinced Faith that she was simply deeply in tune with nature and, therefore, her body had adapted these magnificent colors.

The Council of Elders entered the great hall in the crown of the tree. The hall was splendid, with windows and flowers everywhere.

It was dusted with Pixie dust from three selected, newly lighted seventeen-year-olds on a weekly basis. Due to the fresh dust of newly empowered Pixies, it always felt like spring in the hall. The marvelous sight and smell of roses, orchids, daisies, lavender, honeysuckle, and other fragrant flowers with their rich scent was always present. Even when the rest of the forest was covered in thick winter snow, the great hall held spring in the air.

In the center of the hall stood a heavy oak table, and out of the middle grew a very small cherry tree. As soon as Maliek entered, the eternal blossoms opened. When Mariskina entered, the blossoms began to glow. The elders gathered around the table without saying a word.

They pulled back their chairs and sat down in order of their age and rank, with Maliek and Mariskina being the last to sit down. Maliek had just asked for a moment of silence for reflection when the door swung open.

In a hue of pink light, Chichine floated into the hall. She believed herself to be the oldest Pixie in the land. No one was exactly sure what her actual age was but they all thought it was funny that Chichine and Mariskina had such a debate about it for many suncycles. Only five of the thirteen Council members had ever met her.

Mariskina had always insisted that she and Chichine were within five years of each other, but anyone who saw them next to each other knew better. Chichine also had much stronger powers.

Two smaller Pixies entered behind her. Both of them held their heads bowed, and they were both draped in pale-pink dresses with silvery wings.

Mariskina slowly stood up while rolling her eyes. "Must your entrance be more and more dramatic each time you allow the community to see you?" she taunted, confronting Chichine with obvious irritation.

"Oh, well hello dear, still around then, are you?" Chichine floated past Mariskina, leaving a small trail of sparkling lavender dust. "I'm not here for anything other than a quick word with Maliek." She had stopped in front of him and lowered her feet to the floor. Her wings dimmed, and she smiled at Maliek. "You mustn't worry about Faith. She knows she's different, and she is strong. She doesn't yet know why, but she will in due time. Make haste to find her and allow her to attend tomorrow. She must have her ceremony for us to continue."

Without waiting for a response she walked to the door and opened it. Neither of her entourage had moved, and when Chichine opened the door, they turned and faced the

exit. Mariskina gently lifted her hand. "Old One," Chichine snickered, "you know the answer as well as I do. There is no need for worry." She turned slightly and looked Maliek straight in the face. "Again make haste to find her, but be careful. She needs to be here before the sun sets in the new day." She left and the council spoke for several minutes deciding which would be the fastest and safest way to bring Faith home.

Maliek looked up and out of the opening in the top of the hall. It was already after midnight. They had less than twenty hours to find Faith.

All of the Council members had stood when Chichine had entered. He urged them to return to their seats, and within minutes, they all agreed that a plan had to be made for the security team and other volunteers to be sent out to find her. He apologized for his seemingly hasty decision to ban her from the ceremony, but assured everyone that it had not been an easy decision. He had also expected more of an argument from Faith and an effort to change his mind. He had least of all expected her to leave the way she had.

Within minutes, it was decided that Barask would be the one to lead the search. He was, after all, the most qualified, as he was the father of twenty-six boys and head of the security team. Being 262 years old, he had led many searches. Several of his boys were excellent trackers, two of them had been in apprenticeship with a wizard and had learned to use their dust to illuminate a large area.

Each of the Council elders went to different parts of the tree and simultaneously blew their flower trumpets. Everyone at Windhill Tree knew that this was a high-alert alarm, and everyone had to be assembled in the center of the tree within minutes.

Mariskina called the assembly to silence and order. Maliek floated to the center and tapped his wings together three times, the hollow of the tree filled with soft, barely noticeable blue dust. This allowed him to speak and be heard by everyone, no matter how high up in the tree they were.

He began, "Friends and community, as all of you know by now, I may have made one of the worst mistakes a father can make. I now need to count on all of you to ... to help me fix things." Visibly embarrassed, he cleared his throat and continued: "I need Faith found and brought back to the tree before the next sundown. Barask will lead the search and will assemble several teams, so please see him right away if you want to go out with one of his boys."

A busy hum filled the hollow of the tree as nearly one hundred Pixies made their way to join the search leader. Some focused their attention on Maliek, offering to help him prepare for the evening's celebration as they now all knew that the lightning ceremony was to take place as scheduled. They just seemed to know that everything would be fine, and little Faith would be home for her special event. None of them, however, realized that Faith might be further away than they had ever imagined.

≫ 3 ≪
I Told You So

Sam seemed to have grown at least two inches since she picked up the little, unconscious Pixie. In an instant she remembered the joy she had felt on her sixth birthday when she had found a Pixie trapped in a rose at her grandma's farm. For eleven years she had defended her belief that these creatures were real and now no one could doubt her anymore. She held Faith as high in the air as she could and yelled from the top of her lungs, "I told you people they are here. I told you ... but did anyone listen? Nope." She quickly pulled back her arm, and clutching Faith in her hand, she ran back to the campsite and straight into her tent.

With Faith in one hand, she searched for something to put her in. She was sure the only way she would be able to keep the little being was if she put her in a box or something she could close. Slightly upset, but in deep thought, she sat back on her sleeping bag. She gently opened her hand and looked at her treasure, still lying in her hand, limp like a wet rag. Sam brought her hand closer to her face. She knew the others were right behind her, and if they got hold of this Fairy, she'd never get it back.

Especially Smelly Duck—her brother's best friend. His name was actually Ben, but because he always had a stench around him, everyone called him Smelly Duck. Barely having finished the thought, she heard them outside.

"Hey Peewee, let me see that thing." It was Ben, with Rob in tow. They both dropped next to her on the sleeping bag, and Ben pulled the hand containing Faith toward him. He was just about to grab her when Sam, without even thinking, slapped him.

Ben leaned back in total surprise. "What's wrong with you? Have you lost your mind?" Ben held his cheek where Sam had hit him. You could actually see the imprint of her fingers on his cheek. She smiled, and without giving him any further attention, she looked at her brother, "Rob, please don't let him take it. You know he'll hurt it, and I have wanted one of these my whole life." Rob looked at her, still shocked that she had smacked Ben. "We're all curious about it. Are you sure it's even still alive?"

Sam looked up, and everyone else at the campground had gathered around the opening of the tent. No one said a word, they just stared at the lifeless creature in Sam's hand. "Well, OK Shorty, we will give you some time alone with it…" Rob was interrupted by protests from the others, "BUT you will let all of us see it a little later, right?" Rob looked at her with all the authority an older brother could muster, as he reached behind her to grab Ben. He was still speechless.

Sam nodded reluctantly as they left. Apparently, Rob's question had in fact been more of a statement than a question. "Can you please zip up?" she pleaded. She saw two hands wiggle at the bottom of the tent, and then the zipper went up. In the meantime, Ben had found his voice, "Just where does she get off on hitting me? I wasn't doing anything. I just wanted to look." Sam heard Rob pat him on the back and say, "Down boy, you know how she is with these Fairy things. She'll let us look at it in a bit. No worries, Ducky, you'll get your chance to examine the thing." Some of the others were complaining as well but Rob explained that all of them had made fun of Sam over the years for her beliefs and now that she had the proof they needed to give her a little time. She had to smile that her big brother defended her so strongly. He had always defended her when it came to her beliefs, even when things got hairy with their parents at times, he was there for her.

Sam realized that all of them would do nothing until she let them check out the Fairy. They would all just sit by the fire and wait. There were kazillion things to do, but they would just sit there and watch the opening of the tent for her to come out. If they had believed her in the first place, this wouldn't be such a shock to them, Sam thought angrily.

She found some empty soda cans next to her brother's pillow, sat four of them close together, and laid a book on top. On top of that, she placed a folded up t-shirt. She tried to fluff the shirt a bit, but it wasn't thick enough. Finally, she laid the Fairie down as gently as she could. Sam plopped belly first onto her sleeping bag, and with her head resting on her hands, she looked intently at the little being before her.

Faith opened her eyes very slowly. Her heart was beating all the way in the top of her head. What happened? Where did they bring her? She carefully looked around without moving a muscle. She had no idea where she was, and there was a big, light-brown thing all around. The sky and the forest were gone, and this strange brown thing was in their place.

That was pretty much all she could see and, oh, a huge smiling face with red hair and lots of freckles. The face was huge but looked somehow familiar.

"Hi. Are you feeling OK, Fairy?" the big face said.

"I'm not a Fairy ... I'm a Pixie." Faith stated clearly. She was trying to figure out a way to get out of this brown thing. Wasn't there an opening somewhere?

Sam leaned in closer. "You're a what?"

Faith sat up. "A Pixie, not a Fairy. There are no Fairies in these parts ... well, they haven't been here in a long time."

"Oh, I see. Well, are you OK?" Sam asked, scrambling around and sitting with her legs crossed and facing Faith. Faith arranged herself to sit the same way. If anyone had come into the tent at that moment, they would surely have laughed. It was as if Sam was looking at a smaller version of herself and, of course, dressed differently.

Both of them sitting with their legs crossed, with Faith on the bunched-up shirt and Sam on the bunched up sleeping bag, red hair sticking up in all directions and very serious looks on both their faces.

"Are you the one everyone calls Sam?" Faith asked, looking at her straight in the face, waiting for an answer. Sam smiled from ear to ear, delighted that the Fairy, oh, Pixie rather, recognized her.

"Yes ... yes, I am," Sam replied, and without waiting for the next question, she said, "Listen, there are a bunch of others who want to see you, so I need to hide you and tell them something like—" She hesitated, wrinkling her forehead, deep in thought. "Uh, I got it—I'll just tell them you got away. I'll say that, as I was bringing you to show you to them, you flew away." She was sure she would be able to keep Faith and that she would have no objections to staying with Sam. The thought that she in fact wanted to just go home never crossed Sam's mind.

"Who are they?" Faith asked. She had watched Sam for several days but had never paid much attention to anyone else. Now she felt an uneasy, almost fearful, curiosity about them.

"Oh, it's my brother Rob and his friend, Smelly Duck, and—"

Faith interrupted her. "Your brother is friends with a smelly duck. That's odd."

"No, no … we just call him that. His real name is Ben. We call him Smelly Duck 'cause he always smells. Anyway, so there's Ben and his sister, Angela. The other two girls are Jules and Jen, they're twins, and they're my friends."

Even though both human and Pixie had very different ideas about how this was going to continue, a friendship seemed to be building.

"Are there a lot of you?" asked Sam.

"A lot of what … Pixies?" Faith seemed a bit puzzled by the question, and without waiting for a reply, she said, "Of course, there are hundreds. There is one tree every so often that is full with them."

Sam's forehead wrinkled. "Well then, how come no one has ever seen one of you? I mean, I've known all my life that you exist because I have seen a Pixie before, but I don't have very many friends because of it."

"Those two girls are your friends, you said," spouted Faith.

"You mean Jenn and Jules, Yes, they are," Sam quickly responded. "They believe in you as much as I do, but we've spent hours wondering how we could ever find one of you and what would we do if—"

"If what? What do you mean, 'what we would do'? What do you think you're gonna do?" Faith stood up, stomped her foot, and put both hands on her hips. Sam didn't react. She was looking at the front of the tent, which was now partly open and had two smiling faces peeking in. "What are you guys doing here?" Sam whispered.

Both Jen and Jules turned bright red—almost the shade of Sam's and Faith's hair.

"Sorry, Samoans," whispered back Jules. "Does it talk?"

"Well, what do you think we've been doing in here all this

time—just gawking at each other?" Sam replied, shaking her head. "Of course she talks."

"Can we come in?" asked Jen.

Sam looked at Faith as if waiting for approval from her. Faith shrugged her

shoulders, and before anyone had a chance to say anything, both of them had crawled into the tent and were sitting on either side of Sam. "This is weird," Faith said, looking at Jen, then at Jules, and back again. "I've never seen two people who look exactly alike. It's very interesting. Besides that what is this thing we are in? I would rather be in the forest. I don't feel right here."

"I'm sorry, this is a tent, and we use it to sleep in when we are in the forest. I didn't mean to make you uncomfortable, but if we go outside all the others will want to see you and play with you and I don't want that," Sam said, getting upset.

"They are already wondering when you will be bringing her out," stated Jules.

"See," Sam looked at Faith, "It's much better we stay in here and decide what to do."

Sam, Jules, and Jen all sat on the sleeping bag and Faith was still on the shirt. Unable to do anything else at the moment Faith decided to examine the girls up close. She got right up on their noses and landed on top of their heads. She flew back and forth a few times before settling back on top of the shirt.

"What's wrong? Are you guys OK?" Faith asked, concerned that all of them looked frozen stiff.

"Well, that was weird, you flying around our heads like that," Sam said, the first to

recover. She looked at the other two girls, and sure enough, the two of them looked as if they had seen a ghost.

"Are they going to be OK?" asked Faith.

Sam poked Jules in the side. "Hey, snap out of it. It's not that big a deal."

Jules looked at Sam, then at Faith, and began to laugh like she never had before. She fell backward on the sleeping bag and held her stomach. After a minute or so, the tears began to run down her face and she was, again, bright red.

"What's with her?" Jen asked, seeming to have also recovered, looking at her sister in total disbelief. Both Faith and Sam shrugged their shoulders.

"You know, if I didn't know better, I'd say you two were sisters in some way. You look so much alike. This is just too weird." She got up on her knees. "Well ladies, I'm hungry, and the bunch outside wants to know what the deal is in here, so I'm gonna skedaddle."

Jules, who was by now calming down but still giggling, suddenly sat up. "I'm … he, he, he … a little hungry … ha, ha, ha … my … ha, ha, ha … myself." Her face was still bright red. "What time is it, anyway?"

Sam raised her left arm to look at her watch. "Just around 12:30. Did anyone make any lunch?"

"Yeah Rob and Ryan made Burgers and Beans. Since we are leaving tomorrow we are trying to use up all the rest of the food." Jen stated.

"What is 12:30?" Faith wanted to know not paying attention to Jen.

"It's the time, "said Sam. She showed Faith her watch and explained to her that it was a device to track of the time of day," to Jules and Jen she replied, "tell them I will be out in a minute and save me a burger."

"So, which part is 12:30?" Faith asked, looking at Sam with a very intense look on her face.

"Well," Sam said, and trying to return her thoughts to the Pixie she wondered how she would explain that one, "it's like the opposite of just after midnight. You know, when the moon's up?" She didn't wait for a response and didn't notice Faith getting pale.

"So you see, when the sun is way up in the middle of the sky, then it's noon or twelve, as we say, and that means the day is half over. How do Pixies tell t ... hey, are you OK?" Faith had flown back to the shirt-covered book and sat there with her knees pulled up, and her arms crossed and resting on her head on them. Her face was buried in her arms. She shook her head.

"What's wrong?" Sam asked, lightly touching Faith on the head.

"Pixie, tell me what's wrong. Hey, what's your name? You never told me your name."

"Faith, my name is Faith," she answered in barely a whisper, "I really need to get home."

Sam crouched down as close as she could get so she could hear her. Faith began to tell her what happened, how she had been to the clearing a bunch of times and how Frizzle had told their dad about it. She told her about the lighting ceremony and that she had been banned from it.

"Worst of all," she said, barely holding back her tears, "if I don't have the ceremony tonight, I will lose the use of my wings. They will dull, and I won't even be able to fly anymore."

"Oh, my gosh," Sam said. She was stunned at what she had heard. Sure, she had wanted nothing more than to keep the Pixie, but under the circumstances she would have to help her. She certainly didn't want anything bad to happen to her. "We have to get you back to your tree and talk to your dad."

"No no no. Do you know what he would do if I showed humans our tree?" Faith shook her head with frantic fear, but Sam had already stuck her head out of the tent.

"Juuuules, Jennnnn come here ... hurry!" She yelled so loudly that it startled everyone.

"Wow, where's the fire, girlfriend?" Jules shouted, darting around from the side of the tent, her sister in tow. The three of them sat by the entrance to the tent, and Sam explained what Faith had just told her. Both of the girls sat there with gaping mouths.

"We need to help her … *now!*" Sam announced.

"I have a great idea," Jules replied, her face lighting up with joy. "Jenny and I will create a diversion. We will tell everyone that the Pixie got away and—"

Sam stopped her. "Her name is Faith. The Pixie, her name is Faith."

"Oh ok," Jules said. "We will tell everyone that Faith got away. You can take her as far as the spot where you found her. Surely from there she will remember how to get home. Remember that funny-looking tree stump where we had our picnic the other day? That's where you should take her."

Sam nodded. "We will meet you there, and the three of us can take her back further if we need to." The three of them turned and looked at Faith.

"I can't possibly get into any more trouble than I'm in already, right?" How could that possibly work? Her dad had banned her from the ceremony for going to the clearing and endangering them in the first place. How would he react if she brought not just one but three humans back to the tree?

"OK, it sounds OK, but you can't all go to the tree. My dad will kill me," she told the girls. "Let's meet at Moonlight Stump, the funny-looking stump you were talking about, and we will figure out the rest from there."

Sam, Jules, and Jen decided that the three of them would join everyone by the campfire and that Jules and Jen would appear to be consoling Sam. They would tell the boys that they had been talking to Sam, who told them that when she wasn't watching,

Faith must have gotten away. They would say that Sam called them back, which, of course, would work splendidly with the way Sam had screamed a few minutes ago.

The three of them searched the whole tent but couldn't find her. Sam would then excuse herself and tell everyone that she wanted to be alone for a little while. They would wait a few more minutes and then follow. The three of them decided that this was the best plan they could come up with. Even though Faith was reluctant, she agreed. She was to wait on top of the tent until the three of them were by the fire, and then she was to fly to the spot where they found her.

Humans and Pixie alike had butterflies. Sam, Jules, and Jenny hugged each other.

"OK, ladies, let's do this." Sam turned and looked at Faith.

"It will work, I promise," Sam said. The thought that once again she would lose a Pixie and her proof within minutes after finding one had not yet crossed her mind. With that, the three of them left the tent and walked to the fire. Faith watched from the top of the tent.

"Please, sacred Juniper, let this all work." She thought to herself. Wanting nothing more than to be able to go home and keep the friend she had just met. She knew deep in her heart that meeting Sam had not been a coincidence. She couldn't explain why or how but she knew they were meant to meet, just as she couldn't explain why she just hadn't told the girls that she could easily find her way home on her own. After all she had lived here all of her life.

Even though she couldn't hear what was being said, Faith could see. At the precise moment that Sam headed for the woods, Faith took off in the same direction.

≈ 4 ≈
The Trouble with Boys

No sooner had Faith turned her attention away from Sam than she saw someone jump up from behind the bush. Ryan, one of Rob's friends, had taken great interest in Faith. He wanted a closer look at her without the others knowing. Ryan, a tall, athletic boy with a huge attitude problem would not admit to anyone that he even remotely cared about such things as nature and the creatures that lived there. Everything always has to be his way, and he thinks he's faster and stronger than any of the other boys, constantly challenging the guys to races. It doesn't matter if it's along a road or up a tree—he usually wins. More often than not, the others just simply let him win, because he would argue too much if he lost. He wasn't even supposed to come on this camping trip, but his mother had talked to Rob's mother and arranged it. Maggie and Ryan's mom had been friends since grade school and so were Rob and Ryan. It seemed that Rob was the only one in the bunch who got along with him, as with the others it was often a "are you ready to fight" situation.

He had been one of the guys who had been there when they found Faith earlier that day. Since he hadn't gotten a closer look at her he felt cheated, but he thought he'd wait till he'd get his chance. When the girls were in the tent, he had been just behind it and had heard most of what was said. He had a hard time making out what Faith was saying, because her voice was rather faint, given her size.

Since he knew in which direction they were all headed, he had parked himself at the most logical spot. Now that the girls weren't around to protect Faith, he could have a chance to examine her closer. There was no way he would be as dense as Ben and buy the whole 'she got away' story. He didn't want to hurt her. He just wanted to take a look.

Caught by surprise, with no time for escape, Faith flew right into Ryan's hand, his long fingers quickly enveloping her tiny body. He quickly squatted down and partially opened his hand. He saw the little creature shaking violently, and he could feel her thrashing about. Faith was so scared and angry she couldn't help but cry. Ryan used his other hand to touch her head.

"Hey you," Ryan said softly, "I'm not going to hurt you. I heard what you guys are planning on doing, and I just wanted to check you out before you got away." He knew that it was better not to yell. He didn't want her to get even more scared than she already seemed to be and he had overheard that she didn't like loud voices.

Faith was furious for not just getting caught but for being so careless. She figured that what worked on her weird brother would also work on this guy. She had, after all, come to the conclusion that there wasn't that much difference between Pixies and humans, nothing more than the obvious difference in size.

"Well, now that you have me, what exactly to you plan on doing with me?" She yelled at him as she stood up in his hand. She had planted both of her tiny feet in the middle of his hand, spread her wings as if she planned to take off, and put both hands on her hips. She thought she looked very scary.

"I could sprinkle you with Pixie dust," she said, glaring at Ryan, "and then you would turn into an ugly toad. Nobody would ever know what happened to you and it might be what a mean boy like you needs. It will take someone as powerful as my father to undo that."

She thought she had been very convincing, but Ryan did all he could to keep from losing his balance as he started laughing really hard. Faith almost fell out of his hand, but she grabbed hold of his little finger.

"Look," he said, and he sat upright and pulled the hand containing Faith closer to his face, "I'm not a bad guy, and I won't hurt you. I was just curious about you. Do you know the hard time they would give me if I told them I thought you were interesting? I mean really … think about what you're saying. I'm one of the most popular guys in school, and can you imagine what would happen if I go back to school next week and everyone finds out Ryan likes Fairies?"

"Besides that I have no idea what a popular guy is, I'm no Fairy," Faith replied, looking at him right in the eye.

"Well then, what are you?" he asked, lifting her a little closer to his eyes and turning his hand side to side to better examine her.

"Don't you boys know anything? I'm a Pixie. There are some differences between Fairies and Pixies," she said. As Ryan turned his head side to side, Faith took the chance to figure out just where she was.

"Listen, boy," she said, pointing her finger, "if we can start heading in that direction, I will tell you how you can tell a Fairy and a Pixie apart." She pointed in the direction that she knew would lead them to Moonlight Stump.

"Why would anyone make fun of you for liking Pixies or Faeries for that matter?" she added at the end.

"I have a feeling that would take hours to explain, and you might still not get it after that," he replied. "Honestly, sometimes I wonder how even we get some of the things we say."

"What do you mean?" Faith wanted to know.

"Well, sometimes humans say things that just don't seem to make any sense at all." He started wondering what would be the fastest and easiest way to explain some of the goofy things he and his friends often said.

He had gently put Faith in his T-shirt pocket, and she pointed in the direction in which she wanted him to go while he explained things to her. He felt strangely comfortable with this little creature in his pocket and decided that he would have to find a way to help the girls get her home.

"Hey, boy, what's your name?" Faith looked up at him. She could tell he was in deep thought.

"Oh, sorry." Ryan lost his train of thought and looked down at her. "It's Ryan. Hey, don't you think we should try and catch up with the girls?" He couldn't believe what had just come out of his mouth. He knew he'd have a lot to answer to for this. If no one else would understand him or be on his side, he knew that at least Rob and maybe Sam would be. After all, they had been friends for as long as he could remember. The way he saw it, if he helped the Pixie get where she needed to be, she just might change her opinion of him.

"Well, are you going to tell me the difference?" Ryan demanded, looking at herwith a questioning look in his eyes.

"You see ... we need to go ... that way." Faith pointed in the direction of a small clearing about one hundred feet away. "We're almost there. OK, so you see, the biggest difference is that Fairies have their powers as soon as they appear. They come from special flowers called Inferina. It's a really dark-blue flower, and it takes about seven years from when the bud first appears for the flower to open. Fairies are creatures that don't care much for the company of others, and they rarely hang out in groups of more than four or five. There is a small group around here somewhere, and we have invited them out several times, but they won't come. They are very nice creatures but also a little odd."

She went on to explain the Pixie lighting ceremony and of the danger she was facing. She had just barely finished talking by the time they reached Moonlight Stump. Sam was there and looked very puzzled when Ryan showed up, because Faith seemed nowhere near.

"What are you doing here? How did you know we were ... what on earth?" She noticed Faith sticking out of his pocket. Her heart sank, the last person she wanted anywhere near Faith was Ryan, she just didn't like him, and she never had.

"Faith?" She looked at the Pixie, and then at Ryan, and then at the Pixie again. "You guys want to tell me what's going on?"

Ryan held his slightly cupped hand against his pocket, and Faith flew into it. She sat down, and Ryan patiently held his hand up close to Sam's face so they could talk. Faith explained how she had almost been caught by a bird, and Ryan had been there just at the right time to rescue her.

"But I didn't," he tried to interrupt.

Faith wouldn't let him interject. "He scared me silly at first, but he helped me calm down, and we have actually been talking the whole way. He's a very nice boy and not nearly as much trouble as my brother," Faith said in a rush.

Sam listened to the whole thing with a trace of disbelief, but she didn't want to accuse anyone of lying. Could there possibly be a side to him she didn't know? She shook her head doubting her own thoughts.

"So, what are we going to do now?" She looked at Faith and silently hoped Ryan wouldn't be part of the rest of the planning.

Ryan gently placed Faith on the tree stump, and he, as well as Sam, sat in the grass in front of it. Not only was the atmosphere between him and Sam odd but he couldn't even begin to understand why this little creature, which had just come out of nowhere, had lied for him. Maybe there was more to being a being—human or not—than showing everyone just what he was.

"Sam, please let me help." He looked at Sam, an almost desperate pleading in his eyes, and she saw how very sincere he was at that moment. But could she trust him? Despite everything they had been through together, he had never proven to deserve anyone's trust. Somehow, for reasons she couldn't explain, she felt she needed to give him a chance. If Faith was willing to, then so was she.

⇒ 5 ⇐
The Search Party

Barask had assembled over 100 Windhill Tree Pixies to search for one of their own. He had complete trust in his sons to lead each of the five teams of twenty to the best of their abilities. It was truly amazing that despite what everyone knew had happened they were still all willing to help. Some of the older Pixies were reluctant and felt that Faith should be punished, not as harshly as Maliek had decided to do, but something. It was, however, not their decision. They left it up to the council and her father.

Under normal circumstances, it would have already been madly busy in the tree. There were so many things to do for the ceremony tomorrow. Hundreds of flowers had to be strung up and braided into long strands of floral vines. All the blossoms used for this were trumpet shaped and filled with different shades of Pixie dust so when the Pixies spread their own dust, the blossoms would open and release more sprinkles — filling the hollow of the tree with a diamond-like shimmer. Countless little snacks for the residents of the tree, as well as for guests from the neighboring trees, had to be prepared, and berries and flowers for seven different punches had to be gathered.

Teams 1 through 4 were to be led by Barask's strongest sons, and he decided that there was no need for the fifth team. They would stay and help with the preparations. He also pulled ten of the boys from each of the other four teams to remain, which resulted in complaints from those who had to stay and help with the floral arrangements. Barask and Maliek decided to make it more interesting and told the boys that the floral team returning with the most unusual flowers and herbs would receive the honor of sitting at the Council's table after the lighting ceremony.

Most of the boys seemed content with that, some of them still complained a little, but when the whole thing was made into much bigger contest than Barask and Maliek had intended, all anger was forgotten. It was a great honor to simply be acknowledged by any of the Council members, much less sit at the table with them the entire evening. They all knew what the inside of their home would look like, and they all agreed that they would be honored to help. Each team received a list of herbs and flowers that were needed. They were to make the effort to bring the extras, which might earn them the honor spot for the evening.

Frizzle had taken all the team leaders, who were assigned to find Faith, to the last place he had last seen his sister. A small patch of daisies near the mushroom was where she liked to hang out, he was always close by to spy on his sister, not something she cared for much, but it could turn out to make a huge difference in her life today.

Skuttle, Barask's second son, leader for the first team, was unusually big for a Pixie. Mariskina always asserted it was because he ate sartan root as an infant. Sartan root is used to encourage the growth of snails used to make deliveries between trees. Those who didn't know him would have thought him to be unusually strong, but in reality, he was no stronger than any of the other Pixie boys. Skuttle told anyone who would to listen that he was, in fact, much stronger than any of the other boys, and he was willing to prove just that to anyone who was up for the challenge.

Team two was to be led by son number five, Duddley. Barask wasn't sure if making him a team leader was a good idea, because Duddley was rather forgetful most of the time. Not that he intend to be that way, he just always seemed to have a lot on his mind. He was very intelligent and his mind kept going even when he went to bed at night. There were times he would just wake up with an idea for something and write it down. He once mentioned to his father that most of the things he came up with he kept to himself because he knew none of the elders were ready for anything modern to be a part of their lives. He had proven, however, on many occasions that when they counted on him, he was always reliable and he knew ways to track extremely well.

The son with the greatest character and the strongest intuition was Otly, the eighth son of Barask and the leader of Team three. There had been countless times during which the instructors of different classes had called on him to go find one of the little ones. There was always one or two who seemed to get preoccupied in the woods when the classes went on field trips, and it was during those times that they counted on Otly to bring them home safely. He appeared to be much older than his years, and he was more responsible than any of the other Pixies his age. He was the only one of the young ones who agreed that Faith should be punished for endangering the community.

Flipp, son number nine, was the leader of Team four, the last of the four strongest teams. Flipp, a naturally great tracker, had just one flaw, which irritated most everyone in the tree. He was very jealous of Skuttle. So, it was just one challenge after another with these two and all too often Barask had to step in and break it up when things went too far. Both sons knew that a lot was riding on their abilities, and everyone in the tree hoped they could, for the sake of Faith's safety, put aside their differences.

One other small team was assembled and would search the outer borders and neighboring trees. Of course, they were not to say anything about the disappearance of Faith. If they so choose, they could simply say that they had staged an extreme game of hide and seek for her birthday and that for the last hour or so they had not been able to find her. The sun was already fairly high in the sky, and they all knew they were running out of time fast. They had just five and a half inklies left to bring Faith home, and every resident of Windhill Tree hoped that she hadn't chosen to run away and that she did, in fact, realize how important it was for her to find the courage to come home. Surely, she had to have known that she would not be banned from the ceremony.

Not a single human being could have guessed what was going on in the tree had they stood near it that morning. Standing over fifteen feet high, with a perfect crown and countless clusters of pale pink and yellow flowers, all the leaves in the tree seemed to be sparkling. Had one stood and looked at the blooming tree that morning, they would have thought it was the morning dew glistening in the light of the sun, but only the inhabitants of the tree knew it was, in fact, their wings and the soft humming of all the busy creatures that gave the tree all its beauty. Would the end of this day still hold the magic they all hoped it would?

⇒ 6 ⇐
Three Friends, One Thought

Both Ryan and Sam were wondering how all of this would unfold, but their thoughts were going in very different directions. Faith sensed that they were at odds, and she herself would prefer a little time to figure out what she would do about bringing two humans to Windmill. Surely they would kick her out of the community after that. Nothing was feared as much in the Pixie world as a human being. Stories had been passed down for countless generations of horrible things that had happened to Pixies at the hands of humans.

"Isn't this a beautiful spot?" she offered, unable to think of anything else to say.

"It sure is," both Ryan and Sam spouted at the same time. Ryan looked around and noticed that the clearing appeared to be filled with flowers in every shape and color. His face turned bright red and then he muttered, "Well, as far as this sort of thing goes." Sam looked away and smiled.

Faith had also taken notice as she looked around. "A lot of the Pixies from my community have already been here."

"How can you tell?" asked Ryan. Faith spread her wings and flew closer to the ground, where she pointed at a small patch of a light-lavender flower. They were so small that Sam and Ryan had to squat down to see them clearly.

"See how many are missing?" Faith asked, but without waiting for a response she said, "They are usually gathered for a celebration. There are about one hundred or more Pixies who spend the entire time from sun-up to sun-down gathering flowers." In her heart she knew that this could only mean one thing, her dad had changed her mind. Would she now be endangering everything again by bringing humans? She couldn't turn back now, something told her what she had decided was the right thing to do.

Faith smiled when Sam got on her hands and knees to take a closer look, it seemed no matter how hard she tried, she couldn't see if there were any flowers missing. They were so tiny. She squealed with delight when she finally noticed the missing patches. Once she had seen what to look for, she noticed little spots everywhere and was instantly amazed by the thought that so many Pixies were buzzing around to gather flowers.

"Faith, how far is your tree from here?" she asked while she crawled around on the ground examining small patches of flowers.

"Not much further, why?" responded Faith.

"Well," said Sam in obvious deep thought, "how do they get all these little blossoms to the tree? Don't they have to fly back and forth a lot?"

"Not at all," said Faith with a big grin on her face. "We have these nets the tree spiders weave for us. They are really small, but since they belong to the Pixie family, they can use dust just like Pixies. So, when they weave the nets, they add dust to the material, and when we fill the nets with blossoms, they expand but don't get heavy. So, it's like carrying one flower when the net is actually full of hundreds of them." Sam and Ryan listened to Faith in total amazement.

"No way," said Ryan. He tried to picture the whole process in his head, but there was nothing to base it on. He got the image of a pink spider spitting out sparkling thread

and burst into laughter. Faith, who was just inches away from Sam's face, looked at him, and then the girls looked at each other. Sam wrinkled her forehead, pulled up her eyebrows, and shrugged her shoulders.

Ryan was beginning to turn bright red and was still laughing as hard as before. "What's so funny?" asked Sam. Ryan shook his head and tried to explain the best he could. The more he described the picture in his mind to the girls, the more Sam started to snicker. Faith, on the other hand, did not understand why it was so amusing.

"The spiders aren't pink! Wherever did you get such an idea?" Faith exclaimed, obviously irritated. "They are green—that's why we call them tree spiders—and they don't spit out the threads. There is an opening on their lower stomach where the threads come out." Both Ryan and Sam stopped laughing when they noticed how upset Faith had gotten.

"They are very special spiders," Faith continued. "It takes over five sun cycles for the tree spiders to hatch younglings. Only half of them survive, because they hatch in winter and a lot of them freeze."

"Wow," Ryan was amazed and still trying to recover from laughing so hard. "I cannot believe how different our worlds are … yet there seem to be so many similarities." "What do you mean?" asked Sam. He thought for a minute and then said, "Teenagers get in trouble in the Pixie world just the same way as they do in our world. I mean, if Faith hadn't gotten in trouble with her dad, she wouldn't have run away."

"I didn't run away," Faith replied, even though she yelled Ryan and Sam almost didn't hear her. "I had gone to think, and that's when you found me. I really didn't run away, and I know almost the whole tree is out looking for me." Sam held up her hand, and Faith landed on it. She sat down and rested her head on her knees, which she had wrapped her arms around. Faith had explained everything earlier andshe knew how bad Faith felt about the whole thing. She sat down at the edge of the tree stump and motioned for Ryan to do the same.

Ryan seemed puzzled. "I will never understand how girls can be laughing so hard one minute and be dead serious the next. That is just one special skill to switch moods from one second to the next. I—" "Ryan, please," Sam said, looking at him and shaking her head, not in disbelief at his comments, but more to let him know that right now was not a good time for jokes. Ryan looked at Faith all crunched up on Sam's hand and could see that she was upset.

"Well, ladies, we might want to consider how to get moving, time isn't standing still you know." Ryan cleared his throat and suddenly seemed very much in charge of things and wanting this whole thing to continue.

Faith raised her head and saw Sam and Ryan smiling at her with a look of gentle kindness. She could not understand that everyone in the tree, most of all her father, seemed to think humans were so bad? Since she had met the kids, they had been kind. Yes, there had been curiosity, but it had been her own curiosity that had gotten her into this predicament in the first place. For as long as she could remember, all she had ever heard were tales of her kind disappearing at the hands of humans. Yet, there had never been any proof. Not even her father's or his father's generations had, in fact, seen a human nor were there anything but tales of an encounter. How would she explain bringing not only one but two of them to the tree? How would she convince everyone in the community that neither Sam nor Ryan meant any of them any harm? All of the Pixies in the tree who were close to her age would be more open-minded. But they'd still be scared because of the stories. The older Pixies would be just right out scared.

Maybe it would be best if she went up to the tree by herself, found her dad, and explained things to him. Maybe they could talk a bit, and she could tell him whom she brought. More than likely, though, an encounter would create a whole new set of problems, and today was not the right day for that. Maybe she should talk to Sam and Ryan and tell them that they could only go so far before they would have to turn back. She would have gone with that had there not been this deep feeling that she should bring them along. There would be so many preparations going on in the tree that the presence of humans would surely bring everything to a screeching halt. There just wasn't a right or a wrong way to do this, was there?

Faith looked up at Sam, who seemed to be staring in deep concentration at a patch of flowers. Sam seemed lost in her own thoughts. Her years of trying to make everyone she knew believe there really were Pixies had finally come full circle. It had been on her sixth birthday that she had seen a Pixie for the first time. She had found a Pixie for the first time back then in a rosebud on her grandma's farm.

To this day, she had kept the rosebud in a book about Pixies, which she had gotten that birthday. Sam smiled wistfully at the thought of how many times she had held that rosebud in her hand when everyone told her that she was nuts. Each time it had given her hope that someday she would find another Pixie.

Sam glanced at Ryan. Faith was fluttering around right in front of his nose, trying to get his attention, but he seemed to be off in another world. What better place could there be besides right here and now? Ryan soon spotted Faith, and he grinned at this amazing creature before him. Poor Sam, he realized, she had endured more ridicule than he ever wanted to deal with, because she held her ground for eleven years, ever since the time she first observed that these little beings really existed. Ryan had been one of the meanest kids when it came to teasing her about it. How would he ever apologize being so cruel? Would she ever forgive him? Little did he know that Sam had never been resentful of anyone for their comments. She knew the truth in her heart. He had even gotten more kids at school to tease her, so now he felt worse than he ever had in his whole life. "Sam," Ryan started, looking at her regretfully.

"You don't have to say anything," she interjected, "I know what you are about to say, and there really is no need for you to apologize." She took a step toward him and patted his back. At that same moment, Faith flew in front of his face and touched his nose with both hands. The three friends gave each other a assuring look and then Faith led the way into the woods.

Sam smiled at herself and thought it would be interesting to see how Ryan would act once they were back at the camp and he had to deal with the other boys again. Surely he would not be able to do things the same way he had been.

"Hey Sam," Ryan said, "come to think of it, what happened to Jules and Jenn coming with you up to this point?" He had just recalled the conversation he had overheard in the tent. Sam explained that as they made their way through some thick bushes Jules scratched her leg pretty badly. It was bleeding, so they had decided to stay behind to clean it and doctor upthe whole thing.

Faith looked at her friends and reflected on how badly she wished she could be free of the fear of what was about to happen next and if the choices her heart was telling her to make were right.

≫ 7 ≪
Team 3 on High Alert

Each of the search teams went off to a separate area close to the bottom of the tree trunk, where the security rooms were located. Otly pushed out a knot in the bark to let in the light andsee outside. "We have a tough but interesting job ahead of us," he announced. "We must remember that we may encounter those who mean us harm. We must also remember that, even though bringing Faith home is what we are ordered to do, we cannot risk the safety of the community."

He turned toward the tree trunk and pulled out a chart showing the woods and clearing around Windhill Tree. Even though everyone was very familiar with the area, the chart gave everything a different perspective. It was divided into four sectors, each represented by a different color. Otly's team was in charge of the yellow sector, which represented the west. They spent a few moments going over the area and then grabbed their yellow trumpets and made their way to the first branch of the tree. Just where the branch curved away from the tree was a hidden opening. Otly pulled open the bark, flew out to makesure everything was clear, and instructed the remaining team members to do the same. One by one, they flew out and lined up. Just seconds behind them came the other teams. The four brothers consulted each other briefly, shook hands, and wished each other success and luck.

"Hey Otly," Flipp yelled at his brother. "I found some yellow puff flies—figured you didn't have breakfast yet, so they're in your room." Flipp had been trying to get Otly to eat yellow puff flies for at least four sun cycles, maybe even longer. Well, at least he had eaten glow slugs, which had turned his hair bright purple. Flipp wanted nothing more than to see yellow stripes in that purple hair. Otly threw him an angry look, and Flipp laughed so hard it tossed him into a summersault. There just never seemed to be a wrong time to poke fun at his brother.

"Boys!" Barask shouted, having come to the edge of the branch to watch his sons for a few moments. "Don't you have more important things to do than to make fun of each other?" The boys straightened out the moment they heard his voice, yelling back, "Yes, sir." Barask spoke with all of them for a few moments, wished them the best of luck and success in not only bringing home Faith, but in not encountering any problems. Each of the teams flew in their assigned direction. Barask stood on the branch watching his sons lead away their teams. His pride that his boys had turned out to be such reliable adults, even though they made fun of each other rather often, showed on his face and his puffed chest. He knew very well, and was always the first to admit that with a little fun, everything seemed easier. He returned to the inside of the tree to continue with preparations for the upcoming celebration, which was now just a few inklies away. Even a celebration like the one today required a sense of safety. One would be surprised at what could go wrong. He thought back to one of the lighting ceremonies several sun cycles ago. It had been the wish of the Pixie being lighted to have large garlands of flowers in the top of the tree hollow. The garlands hadn't been attached properly for that height and the whole thing came crashing down with the High Council's table as its main target. Had it not been for the quick thinking of some of his boys, that whole event may have ended badly for some of the council members. Nodding to himself, he again assured himself that safety was very important.

The clearing was beautiful. It seemed every living thing around knew what day it was and wanted to look its best for the celebration. No human eye could have detected the four small groups of Pixies that had left the tree and were about to search every patch of earth within the boundaries of the clearing.

At the outer perimeter of the Windhill Tree community, Gustus and his team had been busy for some time. They had left well before the other four teams as they had the longest flight time and greatest distance to search. He strongly believed in taking part in everything his team did, he didn't want to just give orders and he knew his team appreciated that and it made him one of their own. Letting go of his thoughts he heard a distinct and unmistakable squeak behind him. He immediately knew that it could only mean one thing—a bird. His heart raced, and he could feel the beads of sweat building on his forehead. It hadn't been that long ago that he had lost his left ear to a bird that was trying to have him for a snack.

Generally, the birds in the clearing knew how to identify a Pixie and knew, therefore, not to bother them. But there were a few birds that didn't follow the rules, since they nested on the other side of the perimeter. If there was a shortage of bugs on their side, for whatever reason, they often crossed the line and helped themselves to whatever they could find. Another squeak, and this time Gustus lifted his trumpet and blew. He realized the entire team was in danger, and without their collective maneuvering skills, they would not to be able to outsmart the determined bird.

All in all, it took mere seconds for the team to become aware of the impending situation, though few of the Pixies had ever dealt with a circumstance such as this before. Gustus had no more than two seconds to let them know that the only way to scare the bird enough to make it leave was to surround its head and blow the trumpets as hard as they could. By the time the bird was no more than about an inch away from Gustus, the Pixie guards surrounded the bird's head so fast it would not have been noticeable by the human eye. Neither did the bird notice what happened. But it was too late. In horror, Gustus saw the beak of the bird open, ready to grab its prey, snapping and scratching the leg of Tutle.

At 63, Tutle was the youngest of the tree guards. He really had no experience defending the tree. Now, a bird held his leg in its beak. The trumpets blew, and the bird swung its head from side to side, waving Tutle through the air like a little rag doll. The bird's beak struck Tutle's left wing, breaking it. Gustus could see if the bird let go now, Tutle would fall to the ground and disappear in a puff of Pixie dust as all Pixies did when their life ended unexpectedly. Somehow, they would have to catch Tutle when the bird let go of him. Gustus quickly instructed two of the Pixies to quickly fetch a sirasol leaf to catch their endangered comrade and for the others to stop blowing their trumpets until the leaf was positioned to catch Tutle. Sirasol grew everywhere and came in very handy, since it is very elastic, the leaves can stretch to ten times their size without tearing.

No sooner had the two Pixie guards returned with the leaf than the bird let go of Tutle. No one knew that Tutle was not the one the birds had been sent for. The lifeless body of the Pixie fell at increasing speed. The two holding the leaf stretched it taut, and with a strong thump, Tutle landed, luckily, smack-dab in the middle.

"Sir Gustus," one of the guards yelled at the team leader, "we need to take him back to the tree. He's badly injured." Gustus took a quick look at Tutle and nodded, the two flew off with the unconscious Tutle in the leaf. At this point, they knew he was alive, because no Pixie dust had yet been spilled, but they did not notice he had taken on the pale-green hue that occurred just before the release of the dust.

The bird had, by now, flown away, and after taking a minute to focus again the team continued its search, the remainder of which was uneventful. Nothing but the return of Faith occupied the minds of all the Pixies. However, none knew why her return was deemed so very important.

Otly's team had made its way to the mushroom where everyone knew Faith had been, but it had been quite some time ago. The entire team quickly checked the area around the mushroom, and Otly noticed right away that something had definitely taken place here. He inspected the top of the mushroom and realized that someone much bigger than he had been there not too long ago. Actually, several rather large beings had been there. Otly instructed one of his team members to report back to the tree and return right away.

In the meantime, they would move on to Moonlight Stump. The team gathered for a briefing and then set about their way, the report had been filed with Barask, as was customary when a big search like this was under way, even though searches like this didn't happen all that often. He would be back with his team before they reached the Stump.

They had made their way through the thick underbrush near the tree when Otly noticed two human beings walking toward him and his team. He sounded the trumpet, and everyone took cover. As the two beings came closer, Otly noticed yet a third, much-smaller being, one all too familiar: it was Faith.

Otly was stunned. What did she think she was doing? Surely, she wasn't leading the two straight to the tree? Had she lost her mind completely?

Now, the other guards also noticed what Otly had seen, and not one of them was able to move. As if in slow motion, Otly raised his trumpet and began to blow, knowing that Faith would be able to hear the alarm.

Maybe she was in danger and being held against her will. Even though this was highly unlikely, it was still possible. He had known her all of her life and he knew that Faith could talk her way out of anything. He was not even going to begin to comprehend what she may be doing or thinking.

Though the reporting guard had not yet returned, Otly felt he had to send someone else to give an urgent update to Barask and have him send reinforcements just in case.

Within minutes, a communication chain had been formed between the tree and the place near the stump where Otly, his team, Faith, and the kids had been located. The highest alarm had been sounded in the tree, and preparations for the evening's celebration had come to a complete halt. Maliek found it necessary to assemble everyone for a few moments to let them know what was going on.

"Residents, friends, family," he spoke gently, cleared his throat, and continued, "It appears Faith has been found, but—" The entire community began to clap and shout without waiting for him to finish. "PLEASE," he shouted this time, waving his hand to let the community know to be silent, "she is not here yet. She is on her way here with ... well ... with two humans."

An uneasy rumble sounded through the tree as every Pixie in the assembly had something to say at that moment. Some of the elders gasped in shock and a lot of the younger ones were excited. Again, Maliek asked for silence. "I have spoken with Mariskina, and she seems to think it would be best to let them approach without any aggressive movement. We are to continue with the preparations as if nothing is amiss. We will station several additional guards around the tree, and the Council will be alerted of the situation."

Maliek scanned the faces of everyone. Some part of him wanted the Pixies to insist that the humans would not be allowed to approach, but he knew that was only a wish. Every possible emotion seemed present on the faces of those in front of him. A thought came across his mind, which he had until now considered inconceivable. He looked at the young faces of the community —117 young ones. Most of them had their ceremony within the last sun cycle. Today was to be his daughter's turn, with six more to be initiated over the next few caspens. If everything Mariskina and Chinine had talked about and predicted were to come to pass, he would have to act now. It could surely backfire, but it was not his place to make that decision. All the things he had said to this community, all of the attempts he had made, were to keep things the way they had been for all the years he could remember. Was it now time to step back and allow the young ones to take charge of their future?

Again he scanned the faces of those before him. He saw hope overflowing in the faces of those that belonged to Faith's generation.

In the faces of those in his generation and older, he detected a twinge of fear. He cleared his throat and began to speak. "We can no longer avoid change. If we want our young ones to continue living as we have for countless sun cycles, we will need to allow them to begin making decisions." He waited for a response, but except for the faces of the young ones lighting up, there was no other reaction.

"The young ones are to vote on this issue," he continued, and a slight murmur snuck across the crowd. "If you feel it is time to give the humans a chance, please light your wings." A small bug, similar to a ladybug, quickly flew across the crowd and counted. "There are ninety-six voting for advancement."

"Are you sure?" Maliek seemed surprised. He looked at the bug, and it confirmed the count. "Well, there is no need to count the remaining young ones. Faith is not here yet and we know how she would vote, and six others cannot yet vote. So, that leaves only a few who did not, for whatever reason, vote for this step." He knew that those who had not voted were from very old families and not originally from this community. He took a deep breath.

"So be it. We will let Faith approach with the humans. Otly will speak with Faith before they arrive and figure out what their intentions might be. We will then allow them to approach the tree. If Otly deems them to be no threat, then we will allow them to see the inside of the tree. Mariskina will create a dust, which will allow us to shrink them to our size and will render them defenseless as they can neither fly nor get around in the hollow of the tree."

He took another deep breath and felt his heart become heavy. He knew his time was coming to an end and that he would have to give Faith and Frizzle the freedom to rule the tree as they saw fit. If so, he would be just another member of the Council of Elders, and Faith would also take on the role of a Council member. The number had to be uneven, and it was always male and female taking turns. Had Faith's mother been a member, it would now have been Frizzle's turn to join and Faith would have to wait. Only adding Faith now would make the number even so both of his children would have to join the council.

"Son," he faced Frizzle, "please join me." Frizzle, looking surprised, flew up and landed next to his father. "What going on, Dad?" Frizzle asked while a small knot formed in the bottom of his stomach.

"It's time, Son," Maliek laid his hands on Frizzle's shoulders, "I knowwe can no longer avoid change and I am not the one who can lead us into the future. The way the council is currently structured none of us really know how to proceed. I will make you and your sister members of the High Council today. You will do a fine job ruling the community, establishing new laws to be brought to the Council and taking us into the future." Before Frizzle had a chance to respond, Maliek turned his son toward the community and began to speak.

"From this day on, both my son Frizzle and my daughter Faith will take my place as head of the tree. They will rule together, and they will rule fairly. Furthermore, both of them will be the newest youngling Council members. As you all know, they will be the youngest to join the Council in more than 72 sun cycles. I trust you will help guide and teach them, along with the Council—" Maliek didn't get a chance to finish what he was saying. The crowd broke into cheers, clapping, and hurrahs. Not even two minutes into the cheers, Otly flew into the center of the tree hollow and announced that Faith and her companions had arrived.

The crowd became silent, and in a moment, they began to make their way to the outside of the tree. Some appeared hopeful, some reluctant. Everyone wanted to know what a human looked like.

⋙ 8 ⋘
Two Worlds Come Together

The three of them had walked in silence for several minutes when Faith heard a familiar sound. She knew that neither Sam nor Ryan would have heard the trumpet, but she would need to tell them that others of her community were close by. She got nervous and her heart started pounding all the way up in her throat.

She flew in a small circle around her companions, who were in an intense conversation. "Sam," Faith landed on her shoulder, "I need to tell you guys about something."

"Sure, Faith," Sam stopped as she grabbed Ryan by the arm to stop him as well. "What's up?"

"Well, in my community, whenever something is going on that's very important, we have a signal to alert each other. It's like if we need everyone to come together really quickly or let others know that more of us are close by."

"Oh, like an alarm system of some kind," Ryan interrupted.

"Yeah." Faith triedto smileat him, but it was difficult as she was very nervous. "OK, so we have these special trumpets, and one of them sounded off a few seconds ago, so there are guards from my community very close by. I don't know how many there are, but I want to ask you to not approach any of them." Ryan smiled and Faith was not happy with his thought, 'Honestly, what could a creature as small as a Pixie do to someone my size?'

Without paying attention to his thoughts, Faith answered. "The strength of dust is powerful enough to make a tree disappear. I don't know what has been decided in the tree as far as what they are going to do with me, much less how they are going to handle me bringing humans." As she was finishing the sentence, she saw Otly coming toward her. She could not have been more nervous. The two parties met, both equally scared and worried. Ryan and Sam didn't really know what to think. So, they stopped and gave Faith and the newcomer enough room to speak with each other. Neither of them knew they were only seconds away from the tree. It took all the self-control Sam could muster to not jump up and down with joy. Not only had she finally found another Pixie, there were now many more of them.

"Hello, Otly." Faith wanted to greet him with a warm smile, but she was unable to bring any kind of expression to her face. Her stomach seemed invaded by hundreds of butterflies.

"Hello, Faith." Otly saluted Faith. "You sure brought about a lot of excitement and changes today."

"What do you mean?" Faith tried to read his face, but there wasn't much there, typical for a guard.

"Do you want to introduce your companions?" Otly quickly changed the subject, feeling that he may have given away a little too much and it was not his place to tell her the changes that had been made.

"Oh yes, sure." Faith was thrilled he had even asked. She paused for a moment, realizing that something major was about to happen in all of their lives. It could not have taken place in a more beautiful part of the forest--trees in deep green, flowers ofevery size and color around them, the warm fragrance of the forest hanging heavily over all of them with nothing disturbing it. The bright afternoon sun shining through the canopy of the trees made for an interesting display of light and shadow on the forest floor. Something magical seemed to be happening all around the small group on their way to Windhill Tree.

Otly and Faith turned toward Sam and Ryan. Otly spoke, "You are to keep your distance until you are invited to step closer." He was very firm and precise in his explanation of what was coming, and skipped all introduction formalities.

"The community is aware of your arrival, and we are all willing to allow you a glimpse into our world. Whether you will be allowed to keep the memory of our world has not yet been decided. The Council will make the decision on that either before or after you depart. Your friends at the camp will not be allowed to retain the memory of having seen Faith." Sam opened her mouth to speak but Faith shook her head. She knew Sam wanted Jenn and Jules to remember, but there was nothing she could do. With that, Otly looked at Faith and nodded.

Sam and Ryan glanced at each other, and both of them realized even though this creature was much smaller than either of them, he possessed a strong manner of authority about him.

Ryan, in particular, felt that he had just done something wrong and was about to face his father. His thoughts of wondering what a small creature like this could do to him quickly vanished. He was instantly aware of the strong powers these small beings had. Altogether, it was just very odd. In the meantime, Sam on the other hand somehow felt very strong and confident.

Even though Otly had been made aware of Faith's new authority level, he was aware that she did not yet know, and therefore, he made no indication that she was his superior. "Faith, there have been a few changes you will notice as soon as we arrive at the tree."

Otly remained very serious. "As soon as we arrive, I need you to go to the healing ward and check on Tutle."

"Why?" asked Faith, who came to a sudden stop. Tutle was one of her best friends, the two of them always got into mischief together. Well, not since he had been called to serve as guard during the last sun cycle, but they were still very close. "He's OK, isn't he?" Her voice quivered a little, and somehow she knew that something wasn't right with her dear friend.

"He was attacked while we were making our way here by one of those birds that don't follow boundary lines." Otly spoke slowly, aware of Faith's distress. "When we got to the tree, he had the hue, but I have not heard that he has departed, so please remain hopeful."

Faith felt a knot tighten in her stomach, and tears began to roll down her face. This was her fault. If she had stayed put, they wouldn't have had to search for her. "Please, Faith," Otly said with an assuring smile, "don't worry. I'm sure he's fine. If he wasn't, we would have heard by now." He got as close to Faith as his wings allowed so that he could spread comfort on her. She wiped her eyes and smiled back at Otly. Both of them looked straight ahead, and there, through the trees and flowers, they could see the glow of their home.

"If you don't mind," Otly said, "I'd like to go ahead and let the community know that we are almost there. I will leave the remaining guards with you, and I think you should take a moment to prepare your ... friends." Faith nodded, as Otly gave the signal for all the guards to come together as a group.

"We are about to enter into a new time," again Otly spoke with authority, but stopped and simply said "Well here is to hoping all goes well. I'm heading back to the tree to let them know what is going on here and you guys keep them in line."

He glanced at Faith, who had made herself comfortable on Sam's shoulder and seemed to be in deep conversation with both of her new friends. "We can only hope Tutle's condition hasn't worsened and that the ceremony will be able to take place as planned."

He returned his glance to those who had brought on the changes, again informing the team that he was going to announce them. He flew close enough to Faith for her to see his facial expression and then smiled at her. He nodded at Sam and Ryan and then flew in the direction of Windhill Tree. He wasn't sure what to feel, those two didn't seem to have any powers which could harm the Pixies. What had all those stories been about?

Faith's eyes followed him until she could no longer see him, and she felt the knot in her stomach grow tighter. She had no idea whether she would be allowed at the ceremony. Had her father changed his mind? Was her friend going to be OK?

"Are you OK?" Sam asked her. She hadn't said a word in quite some time, and looking at her tiny friend with great concern, she broke the silence. "You seem scared."

"Well," replied Faith, "a Pixie, with whom I have been friends since we were very small younglings, has been badly injured during the search for me. Every guard has been out looking for me since the sun rose, and some huge things are about to happen."

Sam wasn't sure what she could say or do to comfort Faith, but she felt strangely content and secure. She held out her hand for Faith to land on, which she did.

"Faith," she said, looking intently at her small friend, "I don't know how, but I am sure that everything will be just fine." She gave Faith a warm smile. "I know it sounds silly, but I have never been so sure of anything in my life."

She lightly touched Faith's head, and as the little creature looked up at her and smiled, they both felt a bond that hadn't been there before. Faith explained to both Sam and Ryan that she thought the tree had been prepared for the ceremony, and that she hoped that she would be lit that evening. Faith told them that she really did not yet know if she was going to be a part of the celebration afterwards due to her earlier punishment. Faith looked around, and by now, the guard team was almost out of sight. She knew however that there were still guards here and there out of the line of vision.

With heavy heart, she spoke to her friends. "Well, I have no idea what's about to happen, but it's time to go. Sam I know you wanted Jenn and Jules to remember seeing me. You wanted someone else to know the truth about us and you have that someone in Ryan. I know things haven't been the best between you two but in time you will understand why Ryan had to take the place of the girls." The three of them looked at each other, and slowly began their way toward the tree. They all felt scared and apprehensive. They made their way through some thick brush and then out into the clearing. There, in the middle of the clearing, stood Windhill Tree. A wonderful, magical tree, its bright, shimmering blossoms seemed to give it a shine. Sam unknowingly squeezed Ryan's hand. He smiled,he felt very content with it. Neither of them could grasp how much their lives had already changed. Neither of them would have admitted that their touching hands brought on a sense of security.

⇒ 9 ⇐

A New Beginning

Slowly but surely, every branch of Windhill Tree had filled with curious Pixies. Their curiosity had gotten the better of all of them, except those who were caring for Tutle.

The tree sparkled in the evening sun as the small group approached. A lot of the older Pixies could sense Faith's worries, and some of them felt that she should have been made aware of the changes. A lot of the younger ones flew a few feet away from the tree to get a better glimpse of the two humans.

"We should stop here for a moment," said Faith. Both Sam and Ryan stopped immediately. Ryan could feel his heart pounding with anticipation, he could not understand how Sam could appear so calm. Faith signaled Sam to proceed, but very slowly. Somehow, within the last few minutes, the two of them seemed to have established a strange communication system. By means of simple hand movements, Sam knew what Faith was saying.

Ryan looked at both of them and shook his head. "How are you doing that?"

"What?" asked Sam.

"Well, you're not talking, but you know what Faith is saying."

Sam seemed puzzled by the realization. "Oh wow, you're right. Faith?"

"I don't know," said Faith, "usually only Council members can communicate that way."

They were now only a few feet from the tree. Sam and Ryan could see the magnificent splendor of all the Pixies assembled at the edge of the tree. As they got closer, Ryan noticed that the tree was much taller and fuller than he had first thought. Sam noticed that most of the flowers in the tree were, in fact, garlands of various blossoms and not single flowers as she had initially thought.

Just beneath the edge of the canopy, they stopped and looked up. What seemed like millions of sparkling stars were slowly cascading down on them. Each of them had a hue of glitter about them. Sam's was golden pink and signified patience and strength, Ryan's was almost royal blue, which signified courage and fearlessness. Neither of them was aware that the other had been given this gift.

"Faith," a powerful voice called out the name of their tiny guide. "Please move to the healing ward immediately. Your companions will remain here for a moment."

"Yes, Father." Faith did not look at Sam or Ryan and flew into the tree. As soon as she had disappeared, Maliek flew to the branch closest to the humans.

"Welcome," his voice echoed. Ryan and Sam bowed their heads with respect. "I am Maliek, Faith's father," he continued. "I know Faith has had an interest in humans for some time, and maybe it is time we allowed you a look into our world. As you both may have noticed, we covered you with Pixie dust when you stepped under the tree."

He waited for a response, and both of the human creatures nodded at him.

"The dust is not harmful to you, and you will remember everything you are about to see. We will escort you back to your camp after the celebration. Should you attempt to reveal our location or any of what you are about to see, you will instantly forget everything, so take care not to let anything slip."

He paused, "Sir?" Sam spoke very softly.

"Yes." He knew what she was going to ask. "Faith will be allowed to attend the ceremony, and she will be lit this day." Sam let out a sigh of relief. "Furthermore," he continued, but his voice was softer now. "I have stepped down as head of the tree, and both Faith and her brother will now lead our community." Ryan and Sam looked at each other in surprise, but could not restrain the smiles on their faces.

"Hello and welcome." Frizzle had joined his father. He introduced himself. "I have spoken briefly with the Council, and we have decided that, since Mariskina was able to brew a special kind of dust, we would invite you to join the celebration within the tree instead of standing out here."

Ryan looked at Sam and then at Frizzle. "How?"

"We can make you small," he smiled at Ryan. "You won't be able to fly or anything, you'll just be the same size we are. We will use sirasol leaves to carry you up into the tree.

"Is it safe?" Sam was a little apprehensive.

"I can't say," said Frizzle, with a devilish smile.

"We've never tried it before, but I'm sure there is no harm in it. Mariskina has never made anything that was harmful or irreversible." Ryan looked at Sam and shrugged his shoulders as if to say, "I'm fine with it. Why not?"

They both looked at Frizzle and nodded, and within seconds, a small group of Pixies had gathered around each of their heads and begun to dust them. They felt a strange tingling sensation, and things got blurry for a moment. Neither of them could see above the grass, and the tree looked like the tallest thing they had ever seen. Frizzle and eight other Pixies were standing on the ground next to them. Both Sam and Ryan laughed, since they were now the same size as the Pixies.

"OK," Frizzle continued, "just hop on these leaves, and we will take you up to the tree." The other Pixies held two sirasol leaves, which they now stretched so both of the shrunken humans could comfortably sit on them as they were being transported up to the crown of the tree. "Just sit right in the middle, and there will be no danger of falling out," Frizzle assured them.

They did as instructed, and Frizzle whistled. They were lifted into the air and through the thick layers of the tree. After a second or so, the hollow inside of the tree was revealed, and Ryan and Sam were in total awe. There was nothing in their human world to compare to the spectacle before them. Lights and stars shined everywhere, with Pixies flying around the center of the tree as if the presence of the humans was nothing unusual.

The two friends were lifted high into the tree and led to a long, heavily decorated table. Both of them sat down at the very end of the table as they had

been instructed. Neither spoke a word, and those already sitting there gave them a quick nod and then turned their attention back to the center of the tree. There were plates and cups shaped like miniature flowers, white linens that held a soft silver and gold glow, and more flowers then either of them had ever seen.

Sam grabbed Ryan's hand again, and they looked at each other and smiled. They knew how very lucky they were to be allowed to witness this. In a matter of seconds, a row of Pixies had assembled in the center of the tree and begun to blow the golden flower trumpets. The tree became silent. From thirteen different locations in the very crown of the tree, a Pixie descended to the center. Sam and Ryan recognized Faith, Frizzle, and Maliek among them. The chairs next to both of them filled quickly, and a Pixie they had not yet spoken to, but recognized from earlier, sat down next to Sam.

"I am Otly. Sorry I did not get a chance to introduce myself out there earlier." Otly sat down and quickly explained that Faith had gone to see Tutle, who was on his way to healing, he may even be able to join them towards the end of the celebration. He also told them that Faith had been told about her new status and that she would in fact have her lighting now. Sam wanted to say something, but Otly touched her arm and indicated that she needed to be silent. Chichine flew in front and then, facing the Council members, began to speak.

"Dear family, it gives me great joy this evening to not only introduce the youngling who will receive her honor, but also our two newest Council members. Would Frizzle and Faith please come forward?" They both did as they had been instructed.

There seemed to be strength in their movements that could not be compared to anything else. Chichine touched both of them on the top of their heads, and they were instantly surrounded by a golden hue, almost like a cocoon. Both of them were drifting into a trancelike state, their skin looked translucent, and they, in every way, looked like mystical creatures.

In the center of the tree, they floated in midair, without moving their wings. As soon as their cocoon state became complete, the tree darkened. What seemed to be at least 100 or more Pixies flew upward toward the crown of the tree, their wings brightly lit. They disappeared through the thick of the tree crown and started circling the tree, at first slowly, but the pace picked up with each second. With their increasing speed, the tree began to light up, and so did the "cocoon" holding Faith in the center of the tree. The faster the group on the outside of the tree flew, the brighter the cocoon became. The wings of the Pixie being transformed were beginning to spread.

Sam was in such awe about the whole thing that she squeezed Ryan's hand so hard he clenched his teeth in pain. "Easy tiger," he said, trying to loosen Sam's grip.

"Isn't this the greatest thing you have ever seen?" Sam whispered, never taking her eyes off Faith. "Forget prom, this is so much bigger than anything." Chills ran down her arms and back and she could feel the hairs of her neck stand up.

The inside of the tree began to shimmer as if millions of diamonds had been scattered around it. Sam had goose bumps watching as her new friend became a new being. Her wings spread until they were completely open. They were deep green and sparkled as if they had been covered in emerald dust. Her facial features changed slightly, she instantly looked as if she was wiser and much calmer, and her hair, which had been unruly and wild, was now fine and draped down to her shoulders. The points of her ears became much more defined, and her freckles disappeared.

The brightness of the tree dimmed, and one small light at the feet of each of the "cocooned" Pixies became brighter. In unison, the small lights began to move around each of the two Pixies within the cocoons. Both of them were still in a state as if they were sleeping. The small lights moved upward until they reached the top of each of their heads. Briefly touching the heads, the lights exploded into a small stream of firework-like sparkles, which poured over both of the Pixies. With that, their cocoons disappeared, and both of them lifted their heads and Faith lowered her brightly lit wings. The inside of the tree returned to its original splendor, and every Pixie, no matter what his or her status and rank, began to shout and cheer.

Faith shot up into the top of the tree and twirled with excitement. Then, just as quickly as she had flown up, she came back and landed right next to Sam and Ryan. "So what did you think?" Even though her appearance had changed, her spark was still the same.

"Wow!" Sam was still in awe. "This was fantastic. Honestly, how can anyone act as if this was nothing? I mean spectacular, amazing, out of this world. Wow!"

"So, now you have powers?" Ryan asked with a slight undertone of disbelief.

"Yup," Faith smiled, waved her hand over his chair, and it sprouted blue mini flowers. Ryan picked it up and looked it over, slightly bothered by the flowered chair.

He asked Faith, "Can you change it back?"

Both Faith and Sam started laughing. Just then, countless Pixies arrived in the center of the tree with platters and bowls carrying all sort of woodland goodies.

"You have to try the lavender cookies and berry bunch," Faith exclaimed, "they are my favorite and super delicious."

The celebration continued for a while, and when the moon was high in the sky, Maliek joined his daughter and her friends. "It is time." He gave Faith a strong parental look, and she knew what he meant.

She hugged Ryan and Sam. "It's time to take you back to your camp. I will go with you as far as the edge of the forest."

The small group fell silent, and they all knew this was goodbye. Maliek noticed the sadness, and it was not something he wanted for his daughter's finest day. "Now, now, remember, you will always have these memories, and you will always be able to come back."

"That's right!" shouted Faith. "When you first got here, you got dusted, remember?" Sam wiped away tears and nodded with a smile.

Otly landed next to Ryan. "Ready to return to the ground and your normal size?" "Guess so," Ryan responded. Both Ryan and Sam sat in the sirasol leaves again, and without any commotion, they were returned to the ground. This time, Faith dusted them to return them to their normal size. Within the few seconds it took them to return to normal, more than half of the Windhill Tree population had assembled on the outside of the tree. All of them wanted to bid the two humans farewell.

Faith, Ryan, Otly, and Sam headed toward Moonlight Stump. Sam kept turning around to look at the tree, each step away from it becoming heavier. In no time at all, they had reached the edge of the forest and could see the fire at their small campsite. All four of them watched the commotion for a minute and then Faith addressed her friends.

"I want to thank both of you from the bottom of my heart." As she spoke, she appeared to become the same size as Sam and Ryan. "You've shown a kindness to my community none of us have ever known. Moving forward from today, things will be different between our races, and you will be able to visit anytime you want. Just think about Windhill Tree, and we will know that you want to visit. But be careful not to reveal what you have seen."

Tears streamed down Sam's face, and even Ryan felt a knot in his throat. "I wish I could hug you," Sam sobbed. Faith would only have appeared human size to an outsider not within their small group. Pixies had all kinds of ways to protect themselves from possibly being seen.

"I know," replied Faith. They stood in the dark for a few more minutes before Otly reminded Faith that it was time to return to the tree. Ryan put his arm around Sam, and they slowly walked back to their camp without saying a word. They hadn't walked but a few feet when Rob noticed them and yelled out. Ryan squeezed Sam's shoulder, and they looked at each other and smiled. They both knew they could never talk about what they had witnessed with anyone but each other and they also knew that from now on things between them would be much different.

Faith and Otly watched from a distance until their new friends where safely at their camp. "Think they'll be able to keep our secret?" Otly looked at Faith who was still watching the camp.

"Only time will tell, but I'm sure we have nothing to worry about." Faith's eyes never left the camp. They watched in silence for a few more seconds and then they turned and flew back to their tree. All of them, human and Pixie alike, knew a friendship had begun that would change both their worlds forever.

So there they were, Ryan and Sam, connected by a bond that they would not be able to share with anyone. That in itself was going to create a lot of gossip. They hadn't been exactly the best of friends.

"Any suggestions?" asked Sam, glancing at Ryan, assuming he was thinking the same thing.

He shrugged his shoulders. "Not a single one. I mean what can we come up with to convince all of them that we have gone from really not liking each other to all of the sudden being ... well ... good friends?"

Sam noticed Ryan was looking at her expectantly, as if he was unsure she agreed they had become good friends. She reached out and grabbed his hand and nodded reassuringly. Right away he knew it was much more than that.

Sam looked at her watch, it was past 9 p.m. They had been gone since one that afternoon so they had better come up with a good explanation. Surely some of their friends would have gone looking for them. But the most important thing at the moment was to come up with a story, and it better be a good one.

They could not have been walking any slower when Ryan grabbed Sam by the arm to stop her. "We could say that while searching for the Pixie we got lost in the forest and even though we argued at first we decided it would be better if we worked together on getting back to camp." He looked at her with a hint of excitement. Both of them knew that come morning none of their friends would have any memory of the little creature but both of the being gone for all those hours would still be a topic.

Sam scratched her head. "Hmmm, not a bad thought. So we started talking and while we were trying to make our way back we just started getting along better and better. I mean honestly weirder things have happened."

Both of their moods visibly improved. No sooner had they finished working out their little plan when they were spotted by their fellow campers. Rob, Sam's brother, who had seen them before anyone else, had kept a constant eye on the edge of the forest. He now jumped up and ran towards them.

"Where *have the two of you been for the past eight hours,*" he yelled, obviously irritated but also relieved that they were finally back. "Are you OK? Where have you been?" He grabbed his little sister and hugged her with one arm while looking at Ryan and touching his shoulder with his free hand.

Sam and Ryan smiled and looked at each other. Ryan took Sam's hand, smiled at Rob and said, "Everything is just right and as it should be. Why don't we go back to the camp and we will tell you what happened. It was really rather interesting."

Sam looked at him in fear that he was about to reveal what they had seen, but she could see in his eyes that he had no intention to do so. She suddenly realized that she could hear his thoughts and he was telling her that they would stick to the plan.

The three of them headed back to the camp, Rob in between his sister and best friend, with one arm around each of them.

"Why on earth wasn't your phone on?" Rob glared at Ryan. "You should have a million voicemails and messages." Without waiting for a response Rob continued, "I can't tell you all the places we went looking for you guys." He began to say, "We went pretty deep into the forest but you were nowhere to be found. We did come across this amazing tree though. It stood in the middle of a clearing and it just seemed to have something special about it … ahhh ….what am I saying. Guess I was just delirious with worry."

At Windhill Tree, everything had apparently returned to normal. There were still groups of young ones who discussed the visitors until late into the night. But for the most part, the events of the evening, including having revealed themselves to humans, did not cause as much turmoil as they had all expected.

Faith sat with Otly, Frizzle, Maliek, and Mariskina until late into the night and discussed the day's events. All this was done at Tutles bedside, he was well on his way to recovery after that rather vicious bird attack.Laughter and tears were shared, Faith through thought helped Sam and Ryan come up with the perfect plan to fool their friends, but sadly they wouldn't know where it came from. Surely by now they knew that they could communicate without speaking, a little something she had presented them with as they departed. All in all she was pleased with the events of the day and before any of them realized how tired they all were the first light of the sun was beginning to creep across the horizon.

⇒ 10 ⇐
The Ride Home

S am and Ryan sat with the rest of the kids until well after
midnight explaining where he and Sam had been for hours on
end. Ryan told everyone that he had found Sam sitting by the tree
stump in the clearing and that she had been pretty upset about
losing the Pixie.

At first he had made fun of her a bit but then she let him have
it. She told him in no uncertain terms that she was sick and tired
of him making fun of her. Who did he think he was anyway? He
should know by now that the Pixie was real, or had he thought he
dreamt seeing her?

He told their friends that they had a pretty hefty argument for a
while and that he began to realize that his behavior made not only
Sam unhappy but a lot of other people as well. He didn't really want
to go into the details of everything he had learned about himself at
this time but he would talk with each of his friends when the time
was right should he need to.

He and Sam had just wandered around the forest for a while.
They were never far from the camp and after sunset they could see
the glow of the campfire through the trees. They were just having
such a good conversation and they could tell everyone else was
busy. They had just really not given any thought to the fact that

anyone would be looking for them or worried. They apologized for their behavior and smiled at each other.

Sam looked at Ryan and thought, *'Nice acting, that was all pretty believable.'*

'Thanks,' responded Ryan. *'Well it wasn't all made up. I did realize a lot.'*

'I know,' thought Sam, *'and I know you will speak with everyone to make things right. I think it's great. You've really changed.'*

Ryan smiled at her, surprised that she blushed, and mouthed 'thank you'. They both knew their friendship would only grow from here and they both had a lot to be thankful for. Ryan had somehow managed to ignore all the jokes and laughter at his expense. Now he finally knew what Sam had gone through all this time. Of course it only took minutes until the little comments from their friends started rolling, the general joke was that they had just wanted to be alone and that they has used the constant 'arguments' as a way to hide how they really felt about each other. The fact that the whole thing made Ryan blush confirmed what everyone was thinking. Why not leave it at that?

Before the first ray of sunlight filled the campsite all the kids were busy packing up their tents and belongings. It wasn't a long drive home but they wanted to get an early start in case of traffic.

Sam was sad to leave and made no secret of it. All morning she moped around and hardly spoke to anyone. She packed her things in silence, but it seemed that every few minutes she looked towards the spot where she had found Faith just yesterday. It seemed unreal how much had happened in just a few hours. Being at home would be hard, she had been getting more and more lectures from her parents about her strong beliefs in Fairies and Pixies. They had told her that they thought it was time to take down all the pictures and posters, she was, after all, not a little girl anymore.

She couldn't do that now, especially not now. She had a reason now more than ever to have all that stuff hanging on her walls. She plopped down on the ground in front of her tent, her backpack in one hand, and stared into nothing.

Ryan was helping Rob bag the tents.

"What is with her this morning?" Rob asked, not really directing the question at anyone in particular but looking at his sister.

Ryan shrugged his shoulders.

"Well," he said, "she is rather upset that the Pixie got away. She did have her heart set on finding her again."

"What on earth are you talking about?" replied Rob, if nothing else stunned. Ryan had forgotten that everyone else's memory of Faith had been erased. "Now she's got you going on about that stuff? Did you guys eat something out there in the forest last night?"

Ryan didn't get a chance to answer and was embarrassed to have made the comment.

"Rob?" Sam was heading in the direction of her brother and Ryan.

"What's up?" he asked.

"Would you mind if I go into the forest just a little, I promise I won't go far….I well… I just want to take one more look." She looked at her brother with the hope of the entire world in her eyes.

Rob looked at her and then at Ryan. Ryan shrugged his shoulders and quickly glanced at Sam. '*What are you doing?*' he thought.

'Nothing, I just want to see her one more time,' Sam replied. He shook his head and thought '*girls.*' She smiled at him.

Rob took pity on his sister and said, "Are you done packing your stuff?"

She nodded. "Well alright then, but don't be gone long, and what did you do to Ryan?"

"What? What are you talking about?" she shouted while running off in the direction of the forest, "I won't be long, I promise."

"You know all she's gonna talk about the whole way home is Pixies, right." Rob looked at Ryan as if asking for pity. Ryan smiled and nodded. "Don't you think she's getting a little old for that stuff? I mean…" He stopped, Ryan looked at him in total disbelief and before he could respond they were interrupted.

"You boys want some breakfast? We still had sausage and bacon so I made that and the rest of the eggs." Jules was walking over with two paper plates handing one to each of the boys.

"Where did Sam run off to?" Jules asked.

"Oh you know," smiled Ryan.

"Hmmm…" Jules frowned and said, "Well guess I'll take care of the dishes and get that fire out. You guys still planning on leaving at eleven?"

"Yup," said Rob. "Thanks for the food."

The campsite was busy for the next hour and no one noticed or minded that Sam had been gone the whole time. She came back from the forest just as the last bags were loaded onto one of the three trucks they had brought.

Any luck?' Ryan asked without saying a word out loud.

She smiled and nodded, *'Yeah, I saw her and Frizzle but only for a few. I'll tell you about it on the way home.'*

'Sounds good,' he replied.

The kids walked around the campsite to make sure no trash had been left behind and the fire was out. None of them realized that just a small distance away Faith and her brother were hiding in a bush watching them getting ready to leave.

As Rob, Sam, Ryan, and Jules climbed into Rob's truck Jules stopped, looked at Sam and said, "Do you remember that movie we watched a few months ago? You know the one about the two girls who claimed they had found Fairies and they even took pictures of them? The whole thing had turned out to be a fraud, remember that?"

"Yeah.........why?" asked Sam. Ryan looked at her.

"Well," Jules looked as if she was in deep thought, something rare for her, "I was just thinking of how we would handle it if we ever did see one. I mean, sure, we would know it was real but do you think anyone in this day and age would believe us? We would get accused of making the whole thing up to get attention or something like that? I mean, I wouldn't wanna tell anyone if I ever saw anything out of the ordinary."

The group was silent for a moment and then Rob said, "You have a point. Sam, had you ever given that any thought at all?"

"Well," Sam replied, "not really. "But I suppose that's not something I will ever have to worry about is it?"

Rob, Ryan, and Jules agreed. None of the kids wanted to be the laughing stock of their small community for anything. Rob had often felt he had to protect Sam from all the ridicule she endured because of her strong belief in these little creatures, but even he felt that at 16 she should be snapping out of it.

About an hour after they had left the campsite they pulled over at a rest stop for a restroom break and a snack. As they all sat at one of the hard concrete tables, Rob brought up the subject of Sam's beliefs in the Pixies and how he would like to see it be handled from now on. He felt strongly that it was a good thing that they had all known each other since they were in kindergarten. They trusted and respected each other, and everyone in the group knew that if Rob said they should do something a certain way there was no need to question it. He felt that since there had been a big change in the relationship between his sister and Ryan, the biggest instigator, was now on her side.

"No offense bud, but you did start it most of the time," Rob smiled at Ryan. He in return just nodded and blushed, embarrassed by the thought that Rob was right. "Is there any other reason why we are discussing this so extensively other than that you are obviously tired of dealing with Sam getting picked on?" Ryan wanted to know.

"You have a point, we have been on the Pixie subject for a ridiculous amount of time so I guess change of subject is in order," Rob smiled at Ryan.

'Do you think they remember something?' Sam thought. *'I'm not sure but I think it's done for now,'* Ryan responded. Neither of them had spoken for anyone else to hear.

As the subject went from Pixies to the remaining route home, Rob's friend Ben jumped up. "So what was the deal with the two of you being.......hmmm...let's say lost for so long yesterday?" He had a huge grin on his face, one might have thought that he had just caught someone doing something they shouldn't, and he was going to tell. Before anyone else had a chance to say anything Rob very calmly stated "Did you really just ask that. Have you been listening the last few minutes or even last night for that matter?" Only Ben could be present for an entire conversation and not remember a word of it within a minute later. He just really didn't seem to be paying attention.

"Oh." Ben looked extremely disappointed, but what was he supposed to do, he didn't know any better. "Well," Ben looked puzzled, "now that you mention it, I do remember a bit of it, but it didn't seem that important at the time."

"Ok, then it doesn't need to make sense right now either, right?" Rob questioned Ben. He just nodded. They all giggled a bit at Ben's absentmindedness. For Sam, it felt a little better to act normal. It was hard to steer the conversation away from her time in the woods with Ryan.

The remainder of their break was uneventful. They finished their snack of sandwiches, apples, and sodas and then went on their way. Both Sam and Ryan felt relieved that no one paid any more attention to their adventure with Faith. In fact both Sam and Ryan were thankful that all of them had been made to forget the little Pixie. All in all, it seemed the little group was more concerned with the relationship developing between Ryan and her. That was more newsworthy than anything else…well, at least in their eyes.

As Faith and Frizzle watched the trucks pull onto the road in the forest and then out of sight they both felt a little anxious. How would their new friendships continue?

"Hey," Frizzle smiled at his sister, "wanna go sit on your mushroom for a bit and talk?It seems the two of us haven't really had a chance to talk, since all this happened."

Faith nodded and both of them flew to the mushroom. As they landed on it the events of the previous day ran through Faith's mind as if she were watching a movie.

"So this is where it all began?" Frizzle looked at his sister and waited.

"Uh-huh………," she was still thinking, "I was just sitting here. I think I had sat here for most of the night wondering how I would get Dad to change his mind. I remember the sun wasn't up over the edge of the canopy yet."

She moved around on the mushroom cap and looked at the edge of the trees.

Her eyes wandered towards the campground. The kids were gone and the campsite was left behind clean for the next campers. For a moment, Faith was so lost in thought she forgot Frizzle was there.

Suddenly she swung around and looked at her brother.

"I have never been so scared in all my life as when they were all staring at me," she said to Frizzle, the excitement shining in her eyes. . "I mean their faces were literally *right here*." She held her hand at arm's length in front of her face and continued. "They're talking about something but I honestly can't remember what. All I know is that I was trying to scoot to the edge of the mushroom and fall down to the moss. Next thing I know I'm sitting in Sam's hand."

Frizzle gave his sister an astonished look. "Sacred Batbugwings, that had to be scary."

"It was," Faith smiled at him "Scariest thing ever, but I am glad things turned out the way they did. I just have such a strong feeling that there is a purpose to us meeting the humans. Something you and I don't know yet but Dad, Mariskina, and Chichine certainly know." She looked at Frizzle as if she expected him to say something…something that would make sense out of all of this.

"As will we in due time." He stood on the mushroom and smiled at her. "Let's go, let's see how Tutle is doing." Without waiting for her he flew off. That was it? That was all he could come up with? Faith shook her head and then took off after her brother. Within minutes they were back at the tree. Faith took it in before flying inside. Though the tree was home her entire life, she now looked at it with different eyes.

A Huge Community Meeting

While Faith and Frizzle were out exploring, Maliek had called on Mariskina. He had wanted to talk with her since he was still a little concerned about the contact with the humans. He had heard so many stories in his years, Pixies and Fairies being caught by humans and never seen or heard from again. What he had witnessed in the last 24 hours had led him to believe that everything he had learned was wrong.

His thoughts were interrupted by a knock on the door. "Please come in," he shouted.

"No need to shout - my hearing is still fine," Mariskina said as she entered the room. "What's on your mind, the young one?"

"You read me well, wise one," Maliek responded. "Are you sure all will be well?"

Mariskina patted Maliek's back and proceeded to a chair near the only window in the room- the same window Maliek had looked out two days before, when he had told his daughter Faith that she would be banned from her lighting ceremony. So much had happened since then.

"You've always worried much more than you've needed to. Why do you do that to yourself? It has made your hair turn so much sooner than it needed to." Mariskina laughed and waited for a response from Maliek.

"I know," he said. "Even when I was a young I worried all the time. My mother hated it. I would hardly go on adventures with the others because I worried what might happen. This is different though."

"Not much," Mariskina responded and looked past Maliek out of the small window.

"Maliek you've only heard bad stories over the years. The council always made sure that enough fear was instilled in the young ones so they wouldn't go out and try to make contact with humans. Do you honestly think if we were all that afraid of humans we would have agreed to let Sam and Ryan join in the celebration? It has happened here and there that one of us has been seen or caught and granted, it didn't always have a good ending, but a lot of times it did."

"What are you trying to say wise one?" Maliek looked at the ancient Pixie knowing that she was about to tell him things he might better sit down to hear. She must have read his thoughts, because she laughed and waited for him to pull up a chair.

"I had a human 'friend' once," she smiled and spoke very softly. "I was very young, much younger than Faith. There used to be a little hut in the area where the human kids put up their little homes now- wait, I think they call them tents. Anyway, I think this was over 500 sun cycles ago, I'm not exactly sure, but it was a very long time ago. A small family lived there and they had a little boy. One winter, the boy's father became very ill and his mother sent him into the forest to try and find herbs.

"He got lost and he sat at the foot of Windhill Tree for hours. I finally couldn't take seeing his despair anymore and so I went outside and flew right in front of his face. He was shocked and thought he was near death and seeing things. It took me a bit to calm him down and then he explained to me what had happened.

The herbs his mother had sent him to find were dormant in winter and he would have searched and never found them. I told him to wait and went back inside the tree. At that time, the eldest of the tree was Karina I told her about the boy.

Since she also had contact with humans, she helped me." Mariskina paused, thought for a moment and added, "You'd be surprised to know how many of us have had contact with them."

"I would like to have an extended council meeting," Maliek interrupted, after he recovered from the shock of hearing Mariskina's tale. "I think Faith and Frizzle deserve to know about this, it may help them make better decisions in their interactions with the human kids. Honestly I do not understand why we would spend centuries lying to the younglings, but I suppose the damage is done and we need to move on from here."

To Maliek, Mariskina looked more tired than he had ever seen her. She nodded her head slowly and sighed.

"I agree it was wrong, but for the most part, we didn't have much of a choice. Though Karina was the eldest at Windhill tree, Chichine ruled the area and she insisted that it wasto be that way. She hated the humans, and honestly between you and me, I really think she still does. Anyway, I will arrange a meeting with as many as possible, I am sure there are a lot of us who would like to share our stories, with caution of course. I will have to get the permission of the Council As well." Mariskina stood abruptly and walked to the door. Placing her hand on the handle, she turned back to Maliek and said, "I will let you know when we can get everyone together, after I speak with Faith and Frizzle."

"Well, as my dear children would say, that sounds like a plan," Maliek said, surprised at his own light-heartedness, "How should we handle Chichine?" She was a constant concern for everyone. When she was much younger, she was such a pleasant Pixie to be around. She loved to share stories, teach the young ones, and participate in events, especially lighting ceremonies. The more she aged, the less social she became. Something had happened to push her away, but no one could figure out what it was. When the Council approached her about it, she always responded by saying she had a lot on her mind and she was sure it would pass.

Mariskina flew to call on Faith and Frizzle. She really didn't think it was necessary to call together the whole Council. The two young ones were now the heads and they could make the decision for the meeting on their own. She found the two busy trying to create a makeshift wing for Tutle. After several tries, which resulted in Tutle almost breaking his other wing, they gave up. Mariskina told them she needed to briefly speak to them in regard to a Council matter. "Anything wrong?" asked Frizzle.

"Not really," she replied. "Just something your father and I were wondering about."

She briefly explained to them what she had discussed with Maliek and what she had suggested they do. Both Faith and Frizzle were excited at the prospect of hearing stories about contact with humans.

Mariskina returned to her room in the crown of the tree. She liked it up there, as she was right next to the great hall and she had the best view. She loved sitting on one of the top branches every morning to watch the sunrise. Shaking of the thoughts she sat at a small table which was perfectly illuminated by the sunlight shining through the window in the top of the room. She pulled out several small lemon leaves and began to write on them. The ink of her flower pen came out in perfect lemon yellow. She wrote:

> *Dearest Family and Friends, recent events at our humble tree have cleared the way to share our experiences of meeting humans with our younglings. At our most recent lighting ceremony we had the pleasure of having two human children present. They were sworn to secrecy and we made sure they would keep what they had witnessed in their own hearts and minds. I have to say, they were the most pleasant children I have met so far in my years. Maliek is, however, very concerned so I would like to ask all of you who have interacted with humans to come to the meeting to share your stories. If it does not interfere with your daily activities, I would like to have all of you present on the day of the next full moon. Please return your message of decline or acceptance with my messenger.*

> *With all respect, Mariskina of Windhill Tree*

She pulled a small jar of pink Pixie dust off one of the shelves, opened it and took out the smallest pinch. She sprinkled it over the lemon leaves and within a matter of seconds there were enough leaves for every family member at every tree within hundreds of miles. Mariskina walked out of her front door and pulled a small pink fuchsia off a nail next to the door. She gently blew into it and it made the most beautiful sound, like a wind chime of ice crystals gently playing a melody composed by a light winter breeze. Within a matter of minutes a large number of Humble bugs had assembled just outside of Mariskina's door.

"Please deliver these leaves to the family members and friends they are addressed to and wait for the reply," Mariskina instructed the bugs. "I appreciate your prompt response and wish you farewell and safe travels."

With that, the multitude of Humblebugs flew out of the opening in the crown of the tree. Before the day ended, Mariskina had received 78 letters of acceptance and only 12 letters declining the invitation. By her count, 59 Humblebugs had not yet returned, as some of them had to deliver to Pixies who lived a great distance away she concluded that it would be best to wait until the end of the next day. She double checked her tallies, as she was sure Maliek would want a full report on the status of their project.

Maliek flew through the great tree, searching for his children. He was surprised and delighted to learn so many of their distant family members were willing and able to come and share their stories. Mariskina had suggested that he inform Faith and Frizzle of the responses they had received. He found them in the crown of the tree above the Great Hall.

"What are you two doing sitting out here?" he asked and sat on a branch to join them. He noticed Faith had a worried look on her face. "Dad?" she asked him, "is it hard to be a good and strong council leader? I mean, we've been talking about all the responsibilities awaiting us and we wonder how can we really be sure the other members will be willing to give newer thoughts a chance? There are only two of us and eleven of them."

Maliek could understand the concerns of his children well. The three of them sat until well into the night and discussed what was ahead for them. Both Faith and Frizzle were glad to hear that most of the older council members had voiced hopes that they would see positive changes before their current lives ended. From there, the conversation turned to the upcoming meeting. Maliek had to admit that he admired both of his children for how well they had handled the encounter.

"Guess you've never met a human before, huh Dad?" asked Frizzle.

"No," replied Maliek, "and after all the stories I'd heard I hadn't wanted to until…well now, I guess. All the stories I ever heard were horrible. Our kind being captured, squashed, or never heard from again. I don't know what I would have done had I come across a human as close to the tree as Sam and Ryan were the other night." He patted Frizzle on the back and said, "Good thing I have the two of you around to open my eyes and mind."

Just as they were about to bid each other good night, Faith suddenly cried out as if in pain and placed both hands on her stomach and leaned over.

"What's wrong?" asked Frizzle.

"I'm not sure," she paused. "Something isn't right."

"What do you mean? What's going on?" The questions just came one after the other.

Faith paled and gripped her father's hand, and he could see the feeling of pain radiating in her eyes. She leaned over. "Dad?" her voice quivered. Frizzle and Maliek exchanged a worried look. "Let me call for Mariskina or would you rather try to make it to her room?" asked Maliek.

"I think I can get there but…Dad…please come with me. I don't want to seem weak but I've never felt anything like this before," Faith whispered faintly.

"Well little one," said Maliek offering her his arm for support, "let's go see the wise one then."

They flew through the opening in the top of the tree and landed right in front of Mariskina's door. As Maliek raised his hand to knock on the door it sort of flew open and Mariskina stood inside with the biggest smile on her face any of them had ever seen.

"Are you not feeling well either?" asked a stunned Maliek.

"Oh green oracle no, I feel just splendid." She turned away from them and drifted away in thought, "I think I felt like this once a couple of hundred sun cycles ago." She paused and turned back to her company. "Oh heavens me…Faith my dear what's wrong? You don't look well."

Faith was still slightly bent over and holding her stomach with one hand.

"Did those rotten boys slip you something?" Mariskina asked with a stern voice. Faith tried to smile as best as she could and said, "No, wise one. I just really feel like there are green slimy torch worms wiggling around in my stomach and somehow, I believe somethinglike this is also happening with Sam."

"Maliek," Mariskina took Faith's arm and lead her to the special chair, "let me take care of her for a bit. I will make her some tea and chat with her for a while." Faith loved Mariskina's special chair, the moment she sat down it turned vomit green, butince she didn't really feel like she was going to throw up the chair turned green but with blue speckles. This usually indicated someone was not feeling well and also somewhat sad at the same time.

Mariskina gently escorted Maliek out the door, they were talking, but Faith didn't pay any attention to it. Her connection withSam kept getting stronger, as did her concern. Mariskina, having ended her conversation, bent over and peered into Faith's eyes, as if trying to peer into her very soul. She smoothed Faith's hair, then went to her small kitchen and quickly made a strong huckleberry tea with several drops of maple. Her sister sent her a bottle of this special maple twice every sun cycle. She would infuse it with special herbs only available in her parts of the country.

When the tea was done, Mariskina pulled a chair next to the one where Faith sat. The special chair lifted a leg and pushed Mariskina's chair away several inches. It moaned and groaned as if in terrible pain.

"Oh really," said Mariskina and rolled her eyes, "there is nothing wrong with you, you silly old thing. Now do as you should and provide comfort to the one sitting there."

The chair moaned again and it was more than obvious that it was now pouting.

"Now my dear little one," Mariskina focused her attention to Faith, "the tea will make you feel better and let me assure you Sam is perfectly fine, well, she may be feeling some of the same symptoms. There is something special between the two of you. The humans have a special ability. Sometimes, not very often, when they have younglings, there are two or even more born one right after the other. I believe when there are two they are called twins."

"What does that have to do with me feeling like I ate stale butterfield greens?" Faith interrupted with a moan.

"I'm getting there dear, patience!" The old one smiled at Faith. "I have been feeling both of your energies since she has been here," Mariskina patted Faith on the hand that was resting on the arm of the chair.

"Whenever there is more than one human sproutling hatched, they tend to know what the other is thinking. If one falls ill, more than likely the second one will as well. So it goes most or all of their lives, even if they are hundreds of miles apart.

"The point I want to make is you and Sam are very much like that. I can't explain why or how. I am very much hoping that my sister will be able to shed some light on this, she has met many humans and has much experience with them."

The tea did indeed make Faith feel a lot better. "So you think we're like twins?"

"I do believe it's something like that," said Mariskina. "My sister will be arriving in a few inklies, we can consult with her then."

"Have there been any more responses to our request?" Faith asked.

"Oh yes, indeed," the old one got up and went to her little table and pulled out a huge stack of lemon leaves. "All but five of them have been returned and they will be attending. You and your brother, as Heads of Council, just need to set a date."

"I will speak to him first thing. We were going to collect honey in the morning and I will mention it then. I sure hope Sam is feeling better." Faith got up and headed for the door. The chair moaned, it liked Faith, it quickly turned back to its normal royal blue color. "Sure wish we could have sent her some of that tea! Rest well, Old One, and thank you again." She opened the door and walked out.

Faith stood by the railing and looked around for a brief moment. The hollow in the tree was quiet and somewhat dark. She looked up, through the opening in the crown she could see the stars. She was tired and knew she had to meet her brother at sunrise, but she decided to take just a moment to herself, sit and look at the stars and reflect on the last few days.

≈ 12 ≈
Sam Needs Help

S am laid on the bed in her small room and curled up into a ball.
Her stomach was cramping and she felt as if she was going to
throw up.

"Dr. Holley," Maggie, Sam's mother, was on the phone sounding
worried, "she has been like this for going on two days. I don't know
what to do. She won't eat and has barely slept."

"Do you know if she got into anything on their camping trip?"
Sam could hear the doctor ask her mom through the speakerphone.

"Rachel said that both she and Ryan had been gone for several
hours the last night there," Maggie replied, Rachel was another
friend of Sam and Rob as well as the daughter of Dr. Holley.

"How is he feeling?" Dr. Holley inquired.

"Well, Doctor," Maggie replied, "I spoke to his mother, and
Ryan is feeling fine, so I don't believe it's anything they got into.
It's only affecting Sam as far as I know."

Dr. Holley told Maggie he didn't know what to make of the
situation. Because Sam hadn't eaten anything strange, she wasn't
running a fever, no sign of poison oak or ivy, no rash, it was
probably better for him to go over to their house and take a look
at her. Sam knew her mother trusted Dr. Holley. He had been
the doctor in this town ever since his dad had retired. Rachel told

Sam that her dad liked the idea of a small town and being the only doctor he didn't mind that they wanted him to make house calls such as his father had done. His dad had actually delivered both Sam and Rob, and their medical histories had been passed on to Dr. Holley. There was nothing he didn't know about either of them, so it made Sam nervous to hear the bafflement in his voice over her symptoms.

"Maggie, I will be over in just half an hour or so. I have one more patient to see."

"Sam heard her mother sigh in relief after she thanked the doctor and hung up the phone.The door squeaked on its hinges as Maggie opened it slowly and peaked in, she saw that Sam was wide awake she walked over to her bed.

"Sweetheart is there anything at all I can do for you? Dr. Holley will be here shortly." Maggie sat down and stroked her daughters head as Sam moaned in pain and held her stomach. "Oh geez, I really wish there was something I could do for you…"

Sam interrupted her. "Mom can you please call Ryan and have him come over? I need to talk to him, he might know something to do."

"Sure, sweetie," Maggie said but it sounded more like a question then a response. "You and Ryan sure got close over this last week."

Sam tried to smile as much as it was possible in her current condition and said, "We talked a lot, and honestly he's not as bad as everyone says he is. You just have to give him a chance and listen to what he has to say."

"OK, I'll go call him." Maggie left the room, giving Sam a look that indicated she thought that whatever was wrong with Sam affected more than just her stomach. Sam understood her mother's confusion. For eleven years, Ryan had been her least favorite person and now all of the sudden after this camping trip they spent not only several hours a day together, but they were also constantly on the phone.

"MOM," despite her stomach pain Sam yelled. Maggie ran back to the room. "What's wrong?" she grabbed Sam's hand.

"Did dad *have* to take my cell phone?" Sam asked.

"Sorry doll, I know he should have asked, but with you guys not being here, he decided to take it. He will be back tomorrow."

Alvin, Sam's dad, had left for a teacher's convention two days after the kids went on their camping trip. On the way outthe door he had dropped his cell phone and stepped on it. It was useless. Sam had left hers behind so he borrowed it.

Dr. Holley arrived within one hour after his conversation with Maggie. She took him upstairs to Sam's room and gently knocked on the door before opening it. She peeked inside. "Sam," she spoke quietly as not to disturb her daughter too much, "Doctor Holley is here."

Sam turned to face her mother and the doctor. "Hi Doc," she tried to force a smile. "Did Rachel enjoy the trip?"

He smiled at her, "In fact she did, but you know that is not why I am here." He sat at the edge of her bed and took her wrist to check her pulse. "I hear you haven't been feeling too well since you've been back?"

"Well," she frowned, "it's just kinda weird, like out of nowhere this started yesterday morning." He felt her forehead, no fever. He told her to lay flat on her back and he checked her stomach by gently pushing on it. She didn't react.

"You haven't thrown up right?" he asked.

"No sir," Sam quickly responded, "it just feels like a knot when I stand up. As long as I'm lying down or sitting it's not too bad."

Dr. Holley turned his attention to Maggie. "There doesn't seem to be anything too wrong, could have been something she ate and just doesn't remember at the moment. However, to be on the safe side I'd like you to bring her down to the hospital so I can check her and rule out appendicitis."

Maggie looked worried. "Is that what you think it could be?"

"I don't believe so, but I want to make sure," he said as he patted Sam's arm and stood up. "How about I meet you guys there around seven?"

"Sure, Doctor." Maggie smiled at him and turned her attention to Sam. "Do you need help sweetie or can you manage?" Just then the doorbell rang.

"Excuse me, it's probably Ryan."

"I can let him in on my way out." Dr. Holley walked out of the room. "I will see you ladies at the hospital in just a bit."

"Thank you Doc!" Maggie shouted after him.

They didn't have to sit too long at the small hospital's waiting room. It was actually odd for such a small town to even have its own hospital, but it did serve two other small towns as well.

Edna, the Emergency Department receptionist welcomed them both and asked them to please have a seat for a moment. Within ten minutes Dr. Holley walked in and asked them both to follow him to his office.

Sam loved his office simply because he wasn't like any other stuffy-shirt doctor. His office was full of fun books and pictures. Funny pictures and collectibles covered hisshelves andwalls. There was even a picture of him and Rachel dressed up like woodland creatures for Halloween. Doc had always hinted he believed her about the existence of Pixies.

He sat behind a huge oak desk, which had piles of paper neatly stacked on both sides. Maggie sat in one of two chairs in front of the desk and Sam curled up on a small couch by the bay window. It was late afternoon and the sun was beginning to set. Her mind drifted back to Windhill Tree as Maggie and the doctor discussed different options.

"Sam...Sam, are you with us?" Dr. Holley interrupted Sam's thoughts, she turned to face her mom and the doctor. "I'd like to try something different with you. I know you don't have appendicitis, I have pretty much ruled out several other things and before I subject you to a bunch of tests, there is one other thing I would like to try. Does that sound OK to you?"

"Whatever makes you happy and me feel better," she responded with a smile.

He rose from his chair and walked to a shelf in the far corner of the room. The shelf looked as if it had been made from the same wood as the desk and there seemed to be something very familiar about both. He opened a small door at the top of the shelf and pulled out a container in the shape of a treasure box. He held it as if it were the mostvaluable thing ever.

"Wow," Sam smiled as much as possible, "you must really like that box." Not allowing him time to respond she added, "Doc, if you don't mind my asking where did you buy the desk and shelf? They look really old."

He smiled. "Actually I didn't buy them anywhere. They have been in my family for over 150 years. This little box has as well." He sat the box on the desk and opened it. Within seconds the room was filled with a strong herbal scent. He pressed the button on the intercom and asked his assistant Kara to please bring him a cup of hot water. He faced Sam and said, "My family has been getting this herb mix for as long as we've had this furniture and there is a fantastic story to go with all of the items. Maybe I will have a chance to tell you about it sometime."

As Kara walked in the room with the water, Sam said, "That would be great Doc. I'd love to hear it."

Dr. Holley thanked Kara and she left the room. The cup of steaming hot water was sitting in front of him. He removed a small plastic bag from the treasure chest and with a tiny silver spoon, he scooped a small amount of the mixture into the cup. He stirred it slightly and then lifted it up to take in the scent. He smiled with satisfaction and rose from the chair carefully holding on to the cup. He slowly sat down next to Sam on the small red couch and handed her the cup. "I want you to drink this, be careful, it's hot. I would like for you to take a deep breath before you take each drink to inhale the steam." He handed her the cup and Sam looked at him, she got the impression that he was handing her liquid gold.

"Ok Doc, whatever you say." Sam began to sip the strong smelling slightly green brew and much to her surprise, it tasted delicious and sweet. "This is very tasty!" she exclaimed.

Sam finished the mixture in no time while Dr. Holley spoke with Maggie.

"How are you feeling?" he asked Sam, looking at her intently.

"Well," she paused for a moment, stood up and sat back down. She twisted from side to side, jumped up and walked around, all the while the smile on her face was getting bigger and bigger. She plopped back on the couch, slapped her knees and said, "Hundred and fifty percent better. What was that stuff?"

He blushed and said, "Well to be perfectly honest, I'm not really sure. I have this recipe, which has been passed down for many, many generations. My dad loved it as well, it's like the cure-all potion."

"But where do you get it?" Sam asked slightly puzzled. Her mom was also curious and was paying close attention to the conversation. Dr. Holley got up and stood by the window.

"Well, according to my grandmother, her great-great- and who knows how many greats-grandfather was sent out in the middle of winter to find herbs for his ill father. He was gone for hours and then came back with a small satchel," he walked to the desk and pulled the satchel out of the chest, "full of that very same herb mixture. He wouldn't tell anyone where he found the herbs or who gave him the satchel, but his father got better. Then years later when his son was given the chest, again he refused to give even a small hint of how and where he got it, but no one seemed to care too much. They continued using the herb mixture whenever someone in their family fell ill and it always helped. As medicine progressed, its use was cut back more and more until my father decided that this mix would make a fine alternative medicine for many ailments."

Maggie stood up "It seems to have worked wonders on my Sam. She appears as good as new." She patted Sam on the back. "Ready to head home, sweetie?"

"Sure thing, Mom," Sam replied. She was still looking at Dr. Holley. She knew at that very instant exactly where the herbs recipe, the satchel, and the small chest had come from.

He smiled and nodded at her. She felt almost as excited as when she had when finding Faith, but a knot formed in the pit of her stomach when she realizedshe would not be able to talk to Dr. Holley about her experience. Somehow though, his smile assured her there was no need to discuss anything.

As soon as both of them were back in Maggie's car Sam and her mother started talking so fast that neither of them knew what the other was saying. "Wait, wait," said Maggie with a slightly raised voice, "are you really feeling that much better?"

"Yes, Mom," Sam patted her stomach. "It's as if there was nothing wrong at all and it sure tasted a lot better than that pink stuff you made me take earlier."

"Don't you think he's a bit eccentric? I mean, really, just look at that office. The huge oak furniture, and *that* red couch and then all those collectibles, it's like walking into an antique dealership and…" Maggie was interrupted by a loud laugh from her daughter.

"Just a sec Mom," Sam smiled and shook her head. "I can't believe I'm hearing what you're saying!. This is coming from the tie-dye-room-in-the-basement-queen. What do you think he would say if he saw your hippie room?"

Maggie turned slightly red, "OK I know but still, don't you think he's a bit out there?"

"I'm not going to even validate that question with an answer, you should be ashamed of yourself, Mother. You really sound like Dad now." Sam made no secret about being irritated with her mom.

"You're right, you're absolutely right, I should be ashamed of myself." Maggie looked at Sam and before she burst out laughing she managed to say "I'm sorry, it won't happen again." Just moments later, they pulled into the garage. Without saying a word, both of them got out of the car. Instead of going into the house, they walked around to the backyard. Sam opened the black iron gate attached to the side of the house facing west. The arbor above the gate was covered in pink and white rose bushes. It opened to a beautiful green lawn with the edges on both sides covered in trees, assorted green and flowering bushes. A multitude of flowers filled the evening air with a heavy fragrance. As they came around the corner of the garage, they were greeted by Rob sitting in his blue chair on the red flagstone patio, the grill smoking behind him. The patio and wall around their yard matched the beautiful red and orange colors of the forest, which was visible from all sides of their yard.

"Good evening ladies," Rob greeted them. "Sam you look like you are feeling a ton better."Maggie put her arm around her daughter and said, "You know Dr. Holley and his alternative medicine."

"Oh Mom," Rob said with disapproval, "you didn't let him give her some weird untested medicine did you?"

"What does it matter as long as there is nothing seriously wrong with her and it worked? As long as we have known him I can't believe you still don't trust him." Sam shook her head.

"Now kids, no quarreling please," Maggie smiled at her children and kissed them both on the head. Rob tried to squirm away from his mother's affection. Sam just rolled her eyes at her brother.

"I know," said Rob rather quietly. "I just wonder sometimes."

The group fell into a comfortable silence.The ladies sat down to watch the sunset over the colorful foliage as he finished dinner. The sun sparkling in the trees reminded Sam of her time with the Pixies. A tear slowly slid down her face, but no one noticed. The family sat until well after sundown and discussed finally adding a pool to their backyard.

⇒ 13 ⇐
Secrets Are Revealed

Windhill Tree had never looked as beautiful as it was on the day of the great community meeting. Guests had been arriving for the last few days and there was hustle and bustle to every minute of every day. Most intriguing of the arriving guests had been Mariskina's sister, Helene, she was a character, which in the human world may have been referred to as 'a piece of work' or 'eccentric person.' The best part about her was a huge and slightly frayed straw hat. The highlight of the hat was a lavender ribbon, which had everlasting fresh white flowers on it, they were like daisies but smaller. If one of the flowers wilted, it fell off and was replaced with a fresh bud which, over the course of the day, slowly opened.

Helene always smiled and when asked why she simply stated, "Why not?" When Mariskina and Helene stood next to each other no one could have guessed that they were sisters until they spoke. They sounded exactly the same. The most noticeable difference was that Helene's hair had turned grey. Mariskina told the kids it was because she had been hit by lightning several sun cycles ago.

Helene asked to rest for a little while, the long trip had worn her out just a bit. Faith and Frizzle had little patience. They were full of questions and wanted to know all about her latest adventures and stories.

"All in due time, my little ones." Helene smiled, even though she wasn't all that tired she did want to talk to her sister in detail before the rest of the Pixie world found out her longtime secret.

"When will they arrive?" Mariskina looked at her sister in suspense. "They are already here, my dear," Helene responded.

Mariskina seemed puzzled, "When…How?"

"They arrived while we were meeting with Maliek and the young ones. Itold them to go directly here so they wouldn't be detected." Helene walked to the door of her chamber and opened it. Two young Pixies emerged. Mariskina's mouth fell open. She had never seen anyone like these two before.

"Helene, what have you done?" Mariskina approached the girls in total disbelief. She walked around them, touched their faces and backed away. Both Helene and the girls were smiling.

"They are very special and have never been seen before by anyone except those immediately involved with their lives and education. Sister, let me introduce Emmi and Saralin." Helene stood between the girls and touched each on one of their shoulders as she introduced them. "One hundred sun cycles ago they were brought to me to care for them." She paused and asked the girls to return to their room." Their mother had been a human and was, at a very young age, left an orphan." Helene cleared her throat.

"The head mistress of the home where she had been taken was well known in the Pixie communities of the north and so I was well acquainted with her. She summoned me on a fairly regular basis to buy herbs and dried flowers for medicine. One day she told me about a young girl, who in every way resembled a sproutling. She asked if I could come and take a look at her, which I did. Mariskina, I tell you she looked just like a human-size Pixie sproutling…wild oaks, sister will you sit down? You look as if you had been face to face with an ill-willing human."

Mariskina's mouth was still wide open and she couldn't believe her eyes. She was, however, more than curious to hear the rest of this story. She slowly backed up to where she knew her favorite chair stood. Without looking to make sure she would actually sit on it, she plopped down. That was the point at which Mariskina's concentration was broken.

As she sat down in Chair it turned black and began to shiver. "Oh for purple daisies sake…they aren't scary, they are interesting." Mariskina patted an arm ofChair and it let out a loud sigh before turning back to its original royal blue, but without pink and white daisies. Chair had decided that no flowers might be more appropriate. Mariskina patted the chair again and returned her attention back to her sister. "Continue…continue…this is most unusual."

"I attempted to speak to the sproutling and she responded to me. As the wind blows, no one knew anything about her father, and only very little about her mother. I asked what it was they wanted me to do, all the while wondering if someone had meddled with nature in a way they shouldn't have."

Helene took a break and rose to prepare a cup of lavender tea. While she was busy with the tea, Mariskina peaked in on the girls. She figured they too must have been tired from their far travels.

"Dear, please be so kind and bring a cup for me as well." Mariskina turned to her sister. "There are also some butter lily cookies in the cupboard."

A head appeared at the door "Butter lily cookies?" The girls joined the two old sisters as they munched on cookies and enjoyed warm tea.

Helene continued with the story long into the night. Not only Mariskina, but the girls were brought to tears many times. The girls had only been told very little of what had happened. Helene and Mariskina decided that at the council meeting the truth would be told. It was almost impossible for Mariskina to get any sleep, there was so much she hadn't known about her kind. It was time for the sun to rise before she finally drifted off.

Emmi and Saralin seemed equally excited just having learned their family history. They hadn't been told much, other than that their mother and father encountered circumstances when the girls were just new sproutlings that had caused them to leave. They had both been assured a lot more would be revealed at the meeting. They were also very curious about other Pixies, since they had never known anyone other than Helene and a few teachers.

Neither of them could understand what made them so special that contact was kept to a minimum. They talked until well after Helene and their host had drifted into dreamland, and both of them were rather cranky when Helene came to wake them, what seemed like only minutes after they had fallen asleep. "It's almost time girls. The Council will be assembling in just a couple inklies and I am to introduce youat the beginning."

"Helli," both the girls moaned. "We've only just gone to sleep," Emmi added.

"Well my dears then maybe this evening you'll know better." Helene smiled and opened the blue curtains on the window in the small chamber. The girls knew that sometimes she was bothered by the fact that the girls called her Helli, but she had told them on occasion that it must be something about the human aspect in them causing them to shorten her name, and for the most part, it was rather sweet. Though they never understood what she meant by 'human aspect' and when asked she would just wave her hand to dismiss the question.

"Hurry with your morning rituals, your *Aunt Mari* has prepared a lovely morning meal for all of us." Helene smiled at the girls, knowing that shortening her sister's name would surprise them.

Both of the girls rolled on their beds laughing. "Ahhh...that coming from you just didn't sound right," Saralin responded while giggling.

"Is anyone hungry?" A voice called from elsewhere in the tree hollow. "I heard you ladies love fresh berry tea, and it's sitting here waiting for you with a hint of fresh honey."

Both of the girls hopped out of their beds and sprinkled each other with blue and green dust, which left each of them dressed in pretty blue and green dresses to match their eyes. Emmi's were blue and Saralin's were green.

The four ladies gathered around a small table in Mariskina's kitchen.

The pale pink berry tea was delicious and both the girls couldn't get enough.

Frizzle, in great anticipation of meeting the mystery guests, had gone out and collected fresh honey. Not only that, but he had talked his sister and her friend Ariana into making fresh scones for the guests.

Ariana had been Faith's best friend since they were younglings. She was just a little taller than Faith and had beautiful long blond hair and sparkling blue eyes. As much as Faith didn't like herself when she was getting freckles, Ariana was always beside her to affirm how pretty she looked even with spots. She had always known just how to make Faith smile. What no one knew, not even Faith, was that she had a crush on Frizzle for at least the last five suncycles. She did figure that Mariskina had her suspicions, but the old one had never said anything.

So before the sun came up that special day, Faith and Ariana were busy baking, not something Faith was crazy but she could always be talked into it by her best friend. Ariana loved baking and she was super excited that a confirmation had arrived that one of the oldest known Pixies would be attending the community meeting. She was coming from Germany and was known by the name of Beane. She was famous everywhere for her baking skills, which she apparently had learned by sneaking into a bakery on regular basis.

Ariana hoped to get a chance to meet her in person and maybe even get a little time with her in one of the tree kitchens.

Frizzle had come to pick up the scones and he said they were the best smelling things he had smelled in a long time. Ariana's heart fluttered a bit at his declaration, and Faith smiled at her brother. Both the girls were proud of their creations.

"So I suppose you went out and got honey huh?" Faith smiled at her brother. All he managed to do was nod since he had stuck a whole scone in his mouth. Both the girls burst into laughter. Faith placed the treats in a small bag and sent Frizzle on his way to Mariskina's. He was there just moments later, raised his hand to knock and the door opened.

"You just always know when to answer your door, don't you?" Frizzle stood in front of Mariskina's door still holding his fist in the air.

Mariskina smiled. "To what do I owe this sunrise honor?"

Frizzle smiled and almost blushed. "Ariana and Faith decided to make scones for our special guest and so I thought I'd get some fresh honey. I know how much you like it."

Mariskina turned and walked back inside shaking her head. "I suppose you were hoping to get a glimpse of our guests had nothing to do with it?" Frizzle walked in and plopped down in Chair. It immediately turned bright yellow, had red and blue flashes streaming across it and it whistled.

"Wow," Frizzle patted the arm of Chair, "I missed you too."

"Honestly," Mariskina shook her head as she was setting the table, "he keeps getting more emotional the older he gets. I do have to say you are the only one he still does that with."

Their conversation was interrupted by the sound of a trumpet. Just one blow so it wasn't anything urgent, but he would go see what was happening. He headed for the door and turned to Mariskina. "Aren't you coming?"

"If you don't mind I will stay here and tend to our guests. It's nothing urgent so I'm sure you and Faith will be fine without me," she smiled at him.

"Sounds good, we will see you after a while. Are we gathering in the hall before meeting the community?" He paused at the door for a moment to wait for her response. "I believe so," Mariskina responded while looking at the small chamber door leading to the room in which her two special guests had spent the night. Noises were coming from the chamber and she really didn't want Frizzle to see the girls just yet. Frizzle looked at her with the obvious question of *what was going on,* on his face. Mariskina ignored him. "I believe the Council will meet with some of our special guests before we introduce them to the community." The noises in the chamber got louder.

"Oh, that sounds like a great idea. How come I didn't know about that?" Frizzle asked, but didn't wait for a response. Before Mariskina was able to speak another word he had spread his wings and flown to the top of the tree. Maliek and Faith were standing in front of the door to the Great Hall.

"Good morning again," he smiled at Faith while landing in front of his father who immediately hugged him. "Well, aren't we cheerful this lovely day."

"Are you both feeling…different? Well, I'm not sure if I want to say different, maybe strange would be better." Maliek scratched his head.

"Yes, yes I do," said Faith, "and it's odd, like I just want to jump around and be happy. You know, like nothing could possibly upset me."

"That is so true, I hadn't noticed it until now. Well, I had but didn't really pay attention to it until now," Frizzle looked somewhat stunned.

Without another word Faith and Frizzle flew up to the crown of the tree and they seemed to be chasing each other and spreading dust all over the place. They laughed and squealed with excitement.

"I haven't seen you two this happy, or even getting along this well since you were little sproutlings," Maliek stated with a smile on his face. The happy display went on for several minutes and a small audience had formed to witness the happy spectacle. It was highly unusual for members of the Council to behave this way, but then it was slightly unusual for Council members to be so young. Maliek smiled and said to himself that it was about time the tree had such a breath of fresh air brought on by his children. He also had to admit to himself that he had been the one who had been against such a change more than anyone else. He still seemed in deep thought when his children landed back at either side of him. Both of them seemed just a little out of breath and were still giggling.

"What's gotten into the two of you?" Maliek smiled at them, and shook his head. "It is nice to see both of you in such great spirits, but I did call you up here for a reason."

"Sorry Dad," both of the stated at the same time. "What's up?"

"Well," he popped his mind back to the current matters, "I thought we would spruce up the Great Hall a bit before Mariskina and her sister introduce the Council to her special guests."

He opened both doors to the Great Hall and the three of them walked in. The cherry blossoms opened, as usual, when Maliek entered the hall. "I think I have seen this more times than I can remember, but it still amazes me," he smiled. "Faith, I think we should cover the floor in yellow verbena and drape the upper edges of the ceiling, you know right there where the walls touch the ceiling," he pointed and turned, "well, we should cover that in pink lavender." He turned again and faced Frizzle, "You, my young son, I would like all of these walls to reflect a light oak. When Faith is done with the lavender, please add long strands of ivy and pale yellow roses."

Both Faith and Frizzle loved their assigned duties and went to work. Maliek walk slowly around the room, touching almost every chair. Each touch seemed to bring a different memory for him. Half way around the room he stopped. "Kids," he had a smile on his face from ear to ear, "I have a great idea. None of us have gotten dressed up for anything in forever. What do you think we all really go all outfor this one?

Faith squealed with delight.

"That is a great idea dad." She clapped her hands, flew up, and twirled. Her red hair surrounded her head like a halo. Just as quickly as she had gone up, she came back down, almost knocking her father over. She smacked both of her hands against her dad's chest and said: "Dad it's Autumn, let's change all these decorations and make it as it is outside. We could even accent everything with gold dust and sparkles. Wouldn't that be beautiful?"

"Are you serious?" Frizzle chimed in, "After all the work we just did, not to mention we don't really have a lot of time left, especially if we have to get all cleaned up and stuff." Frizzle, obviously annoyed that no one paid any attention to him, plopped in a chair and waited.

Maliek and Faith seemed to ignore Frizzle. Faith couldn't stand still she was so full of excitement. She bounced up and down as if she was waiting for the best answer ever.

"Actually that does sound wonderful. I don't know how you get me to agree to these things some times," Maliek scratched his head, "but I like it and I think you can pull it

off. If you seem to run short on time, I can send a few more of the younglings up to help."

Maliek left the two of them to their work and went to his own little home in the tree. Even he seemed to have a bounce to his step. He looked through his closet and decided that there was no color better for him than royal blue. But he wore it almost daily, he wanted something special for this occasion. He chose a dark orange uniform, one that had belonged to his great-great grandfather. He didn't think his children had ever seen him in it. He would think about it for a bit. He stood by his small window wrapped in a snuggly soft towel the tree spiders had made for him on his last birthday. Slowly, but surely, a thought crept into his mind. Would it be wonderful if Sam could be here for this?

It would surely mean a lot to Faith and Frizzle if Sam could share the experience. He summoned a skrill bug, a very small pink bug, which the Pixies use to deliver messages to others in the tree. Every Pixie in the community had one in their room. He began telling the bug the message and halfway through changed his mind. It would be nice to have the human kids here, but there was no way they could get the message to Sam and Ryan in time. Much less get them here that fast, he really wasn't sure about the rules humans had about their kids leaving their homes.

"Hmmmm…what to do?" he asked himself, "Maybe it could be arranged to have them here tomorrow, after all the hoopla had died down." He tapped the small pointed branch he used to write with on the lemon leave. Hadn't Faith said the kids lived about inkling away from them? For Pixies that was only 1/3 the distance in flight time. The meeting wouldn't start for another inkling and then at least half inkling would be used to go over the most important things before they opened the event to the rest of the guests and community. It could be done. He sent the bug to Barask and then Mariskina and waited for their response. He knew Mariskina would be delighted and the return of the bug confirmed that. Barask didn't send message the same way, he came to see Maliek in person.

"Any idea on how to pull this off?" Barask asked.

"Would it be possible to send two of your boys? How hard would it be for them to find the kids?" Maliek seemed more excited than he had been in years.

"I could send Otly and Duddly, with their combined strengths they should be able to

find the kids or at least one of them fairly quickly? Does Faith know?" Barask never thought to question the idea, that in itself surprised him later.

"Are you sure Duddly is a good choice?" Maliek looked concerned, "No, Faith doesn't know and I'd like to keep it that way. I just thought it would be a nice surprise."

"Ok then, sir, I will send the boys on their way and don't worry about Duddly he has improved a lot." Barask opened the door.

"Barask," Maliek called after him, "have the boys take a Sirasol leaf and some of the dust Mariskina had made to shrink them."

Barask nodded and in no time at all two Pixies were on their way to the small town where the humans resided. To anyone observing the two it, would merely have looked like a leaf flying through the air.

≈ 14 ≈
Chichine's Evil Plan

Only several feet from Windhill Tree, something evil was being planned. High up in the crown of a tree, Chichine stood on a branch. On the branches just below her sat several large crows. Under normal circumstances the crows would have looked at her as a snack, but Chichine had made a very special pixie dust and lured the birds with seeds covered in the dust. By eating the seeds, the birds were under her spell.

She had tried this once before and was sure it would work again, this time with more birds and a little stronger dust. Everyone had believed that the attack on Tutle had been a mere accident. Just a bird passing the boundary lines, no one had suspected her. The plan had not quite worked the way she had wanted to, she hadn't wanted to harm Tutle, it was Faith she was after.

This time it wouldn't matter if they got the right or the wrong Pixie, this time she would take care of Faith herself while the birds got rid of the others. By the time the pixie dust she had fed them wore off, most of the Windhill Tree community would be destroyed and those surviving would blame the birds.

She hadn't always been this way, she had been one of the great teachers in the national Pixie community. She had always been kind and understanding and loved nothing more than to teach the younglings. Then, several suncycles before Faith was born, she began having dreams.

The dreams showed her things to come and it made her more and more irritated. She withdrew from the community and eventually chose a tree of her own. She denied all communities and no longer considered herself part of any family. Not only did the dreams continue, but they became more detailed and stronger. The more time passed, the more angry and isolated she became. She would make occasional appearances at tree community meetings and more often than not, she would fail to make a good impression or offer help for anything.

There had been days that she felt she could undo all the damage she had done, but she never acted on those thoughts.

Over time she never gave regret a second thought.

Now here she was with these crows planning to destroy all of those whom she had deeply cared about at one time, maybe she still did, but those feeling were buried too deep for her to even recognize anymore.

She told the crows that over the next inkling many Pixies would be arriving. None of them should be attacked during that time. Once everyone was inside the tree they would be easy prey. She let them know that two other Pixies were working with her and would be releasing a net once everyone was inside the tree. She was going to let the birds know where and when they could safely enter to have their pick of the little creatures.

She still wasn't sure that the plan was 100 percent foolproof. The dust she had created to put Abby and Polly under her spell had never been tried before. What would she do if the dust wore off before the task was complete? She had tried it on the birds many times. The dust kept them under her spell for two to three days, always enough time to do what she needed them to do. She thought it was somewhat odd that no one at Windhill tree had ever suspected anything.

Abby and Polly sat in the grass at the base of Windhill Tree. They had been sitting there since just after Chichine had sprinkled that odd dust on them. She had explained to both of them that they were to go to the tree spiders and get a large net. They were to take the net to the top of Windhill Tree and release it when they saw the first bird leave the tree across from theirs. Yes, it seemed that everything would fall into place.

⁂

Chinchinejust kept talking to them, but neither of the young Pixies had a clue as to what she was talking about, but they both knew it wasn't good.

The dust she has sprinkled on them tasted nasty, but nothing happened. Neither of them said anything, they figured not arguing or mentioning it would be best. Over an inkling had passed and still nothing.

"Abby, I would bet my wings on the fact that she is up to something. What is she doing up there with all those birds?" she stared at her friend. "She knows none of us like those birds." With that, she looked up at the tree and seemed in a trance for a moment.

Without waiting for a response from Abby she flew up a few feet.

"I am going to talk to Maliek, or Faith, or someone. We have to do something. She is up to something and I have a feeling it's no good. She has an evil plan with all of the guests are here." Polly looked at her friend, fear filling her eyes.

"ABBY, are you listening to me?" Polly looked at her friend, darted down next to her, grabbed her by her shoulders and shook her. She quickly snapped out of it.

Abby looked at her lifelong friend, wrinkled her forehead with great concern and very quietly said, "I cannot believe she would conspire with the crows. She is one of us, what is wrong with her?"

Polly nodded, "So you agree that we need to go to talk to someone?" Abby flew up into the canopy of the tree, her friend was close behind her. Both of them came to a dead stop in the center of the tree, there was so much commotion, visitors arriving left and right and the tree seemed to be full with Pixies from top to bottom. There was laughter and conversation on every branch and in every part of the tree.

"Yeah this isn't gonna be easy," Abby looked at her companion, "there are at least three times more Pixies than we normally have."

"Do you think we should split up?"

"No, no, please, let's stay together," Polly seemed a little worried, "what if she figures out that the dust didn't work?"

"It's ok," Abby assured her, "we'll do it together."

The two of them made their way through the tree, stopping here and there to inquire where any of the high council members may be found. It seemed to take forever for anyone to be able to tell them anything. Finally Abby noticed Frizzle leaving the great hall.

"FRIZZLE.....FRIZZLE!" she yelled, but he didn't seem to hear. She grabbed Polly by the wrist and darted up through the center of the tree. She landed more or less on top of Frizzle, who had unexpectedly taken a step back.

By the time arms, legs, and wings were sorted out, Frizzle was back on his feet.

"What in the world is wrong with you?" He gave both of them dirty looks while he straightened himself out. Abby had finally let go of Polly's wrist and wasn't sure what to say. Had Frizzle been by himself, it would have been easy but there were at least ten other Pixies within hearing range.

"Well if you have nothing to say than I may at least expect an apology for being run over!" Frizzle was obviously upset, not just about being run over but by being run over by two girls. Abby remained standing in front of him and staring as if she had been frozen in time. Frizzle shook his head and started walking away, the small group standing around him followed.

They couldn't have been more the ten paces away when Abby without thinking yelled "Chichine is planning an attack with the birds sometime during the meeting!" She knew she had said it and within a second she could feel that every Pixie had stopped what they were doing and stared at her. Frizzle stopped and slowly turned. For a moment it seemed everyone and everything was moving in slow motion.

Frizzle didn't bother to walk to reach Abby. It seemed one second he was in one place and the next he was back in front of her. "What did you say? How dare you accuse one of the oldest of our community?"

"She's not lying, it's the truth," Polly's voice was barely noticeable. Frizzle's nose was almost touching Abby's as Polly spoke. "Frizzle, I swear to you by everything that is important to our community, she is speaking the truth. Chichine is in a tree not 500 paces from here with at least twenty black crows. She dusted them with something she used before and she plans to attack while everyone is at the community meeting. She lured Abby and me to the tree and ...," someone was behind Polly and interrupted her.

"Why don't we take this conversation to the Council chambers?" Faith and Mariskina suggested almost simultaneously. Mariskina and Maliek had appeared out of almost nowhere. A large crowd had gathered around the little group and most of them looked more than a little afraid. Some of them began to shout as Faith, Frizzle, Mariskina, Abby, and Polly took off.

"Should we sound the alarm?"

"Should we hide?"

"What do you want us to do?"

"The council would like for you to all stay calm and continue on with the preparations as if nothing were wrong," Maliek was floating in the crown of the tree just next to the balcony of the great hall. "If we sound the alarm, she will surely hear it and she will know that we are on to her. Allow the council members to get all the information we need to come up with aplan. I assure you, my dear family and friends, there is nothing to worry about."

It was amazing how much everyone in the tree trusted Maliek. Everyone went straight back to what they had been doing before. Within just what seemed like seconds, the council members had assembled in the chambers next to the great hall. Mariskina called her sister to attend since she was familiar with such hairy situations. Abby and Polly felt somewhat intimidated and scared but Faith assured them that anything they could share and tell them about would be of great help.

Abby and Polly told them how they had been assigned to go gather oak leaves for the decorations along the outside of the great hall. They had barely left Windhill Tree when Chichine summoned them to follow her. They did as they had been told and next thing either of them knew they had been sprinkled with a very dry and dense dust.

"It is almost like that stuff they use in the kitchen when they are baking," Abby stated as she was lightly scratching her head.

They told how nasty it had tasted and that Chichine must have expected something to happen because she didn't say anything for a while. When she had been sure there was some sort of affect she continued to tell the two Pixies that they were to go to the tree spiders and get a net large enough to cover the tree. Neither of them had the courage to ask why.

They told the Council about the number of birds and every Pixie knew how much the crows loved to snack on Pixies. Abby added that this was not the first time Chichine had used the birds to attack, in fact that was how Tutle had been hurt.

"Did she say that to you?" Frizzle wanted to know. "Well she sort of mumbled something along the line that the birds hadn't done any good the first time, that they had mistaken Tutle for Faith." Polly confessed, "She seemed to be waiting on that dust she sprinkled on us to take some sort of affect and mumbled all kinds of stuff."

Frizzle asked Maliek to go bring Barask and some of his boys to the chambers in a hurry. They were back in no time at all and the small group began to plot how to stop Chichine, her plan, and the birds. As the Council and security Pixies were planning, they sent Abby and Polly to the tree spiders to get the net as Chichine had instructed.

≥ 15 ≤

Sam and Ryan
Go to the Meeting

After a short 30 minute flight, Otly and Duddly arrived in Battle Ground. They split up, one to look for Sam, the other to look for Ryan. As both of them carried trumpets they agreed to sound a "found" alarm to let the other know that they had found the one they were looking for. Otly knew, from what little he had learned from Sam, that this particular day was what the humans called Monday and that all of the younglings who were Sam's age and younger would be at a gathering place called school. Lucky for the two pixies, it was a small town and it didn't take them long to find the school. Not more than five minutes after they arrived, a bell rang and within minutes countless kids poured out of the buildings.

"I was just about to ask you how we would find the kids," Duddly smiled at Otly.

He smiled back, shook his head and scanned the crowd of kids. None of them looked familiar.

"I think we might want to try and get just a little closer," Duddly suggested to Otly. He nodded and they moved forward scanning faces again, Otly saw Ryan. Now all he needed to do was get his attention. The Pixies didn't want to risk being seen, but they did need to get the boy's attention.

Otly began thinking as *loud* as he could 'RYAN….RYAN.' It took several tries before the boy began to look around. First he thought Sam was calling to him, but Otly quickly identified himself. Ryan asked if everything was ok with Faith and everyone at

the tree. Otly assured him that everything was fine and wondered if there was somewhere they could speak. He let him know that they were under orders to talk to him and Sam. Ryan directed the two Pixies to his car.

They met there a few minutes later. Ryan got in and left the window open wide enough for the two little creatures to enter. Once they did, he pulled out his cell phone and pretended to be speaking on it rather than talking to nothing.

"What's up guys? Aren't you worried someone will see you?" he asked Otly. "Not at

all." The Pixie responded. "Maliek sent us to collect you and Sam. We are holding a special event. Apparently a lot of Pixies have…"

"Wait, what?" Ryan interrupted. "You are supposed to get Sam and me for what?"

"Well as I was about to say," Otly continued, "everyone at the tree is preparing for a huge meeting. Pixies from all over the country and even some from other parts of the world are coming. It seems that all that stuff we had been told about human and Pixie encounters has been stories made up to prevent us from purposely meeting humans."

"So what are Sam and I supposed to do?" Ryan looked at the two guards and shrugged his shoulders. Duddly inspected the car stereo, which was quietly playing *….we weren't born to follow, you have to stand up for what you believe…* "Guess Sam has been trying to get a lot of people to believe that for a long time," Ryan said in a moment of reflection.

"Maliek thought that you and Sam being at the tree was such a huge step forward for our community that he wants to include you in the celebration." Otly paused, "we brought Sirasol leaves and that special dust Mariskina had made when you were at the tree."

Ryan pulled the phone from his ear and now actually called Sam. He asked if her and Rob where on their way home yet or could they meet him at his car for a few minutes. He then went on to explain to Sam who he had in the car with him and why. Otly and Duddly could hear Sam's voice at the other end. Both of them flew around the hand holding the cell phone and inspecting it with great curiosity. Only moments later a black truck pulled up behind Ryan's car and Sam hoped out.

She spoke to her brother Rob for a moment and seemed to be in Ryan's passenger seat within a second or two. She quickly greeted Otly and Duddly and told them that she couldn't believe what Ryan had told her and asked how they planned to pull all that off.

Duddly smiled and before Otly had a chance to say anything he blurted out "We brought Sirasol leaves and we are going to shrink you."

"Hmmm….ok," said Sam as a thought crawled into her head, "how long will we be gone? We can't just leave for hours and not tell our parents. We do have some rules, you know."

"I think we should talk to your mom," Ryan intersected," I think that if we talk to her without giving their secret away she will trust us." Otly let both of them know that whatever they did, it had to be fast since they had to get back to the tree quickly. Sam pulled her phone out of her backpack and called her mom. She asked where she was and if she had a minute to talk in person. As she appeared to be fairly close, Ryan, Sam, and the two Pixies headed off to meet Maggie.

When they arrived at a coffee shop, Sam and Ryan hoped out of the car after Ryan told the Pixies to stay hidden.

"Hi Mom," Sam smiled and hugged her mother. "Mom, how much do you trust me?"

Maggie looked puzzled, "Oh no, what are you two up to?"

"I need to do something that I can't talk about. I promise it is nothing bad or illegal but I may be gone for several hours and not be back till dark."

"I don't know Sam, why can't you tell me where you are going?" Maggie looked concerned and not in the least bit happy. Sam got a sinking feeling in her stomach, was this going to be harder then she thought? "Mom please," she begged, "Ryan will be with me and we won't be getting into any trouble…I promise."

It was obvious on Maggie's face that she didn't like the thought of lettingher daughter go off with a boy for hours on end. Especially a boy whom, up until a few days ago she didn't even like. She was still in thought when Rob's truck pulled into the parking lot next to Ryan's car.

"Hey guys what's up?" he yelled as he hopped out of the truck.

He was quickly brought up to speed with what was going on and what Sam and Ryan were planning to do.

"What's up?" he looked Ryan.

Ryan knew very well that if he disclosed any part of what he knew he would quickly forget everything. "I have no clue what is going on," he lied. "She said she had to go do something and asked me to take her. I told her not without getting the ok from her Mom."

"Hmmmm…"Rob looked at his sister and mother.

Thinking quickly Ryan looked at Rob and said "Rob, maybe you should take her to do whatever it is."

"I can't," Rob responded, still looking puzzled, "I have to be at work in less than an hour." Very decisively Rob turned towards Ryan, grabbed him by his shoulders and got right in his face: "You swear you aren't up to anything bad and you will take care of my sister with your life if need be?"

Ryan nodded, turned cherry red, and it took everything in him not to burst out laughing. "Man, I swear nothing will happen, my phone will be on constantly and we are just checking something out, as far as I know." He almost blew it, he almost let something slip, but luckily Rob hadn't paid that much attention.

"Hey Mom," he walked over to his mother and sister.

"Rob," Sam greeted him, "will you explain to mom that it will be perfectly fine." Rob had told her several times in the last few days that he was glad that her and Ryan had become such good friends, he had to know there was nothing to worry about.

Still somewhat reluctant, but feeling a bit better, Maggie gave in after instructing both her daughter and Ryan that they better check in now and then, actually as often as every hour or so. They both promised, not really being sure how they would do that. They got in the car and started back toward the road in the direction of the woods and their familiar camping grounds.

"Where do you think we should leave the car?" Ryan asked Sam. She shrugged her shoulders. She looked at Otly, who had comfortably placed himself on the dashboard,

looking more like a hood ornament than anything else. "I have a question for you as well," Ryan said, "when you shrink us can you shrink our phones as well?"

Otly thought for a moment, he pulled out the small bag containing the dust he would use to shrink them. "I think there is enough here to shrink you both, this vehicle, which I must add, is very awesome, and anything else, within reason." Satisfied with his response he grinned at the kids. "If you have a place where you can hide the vehicle, you can stop there. We can then shrink it and you both."

"What about our phones?" Sam insisted, "We do need to check in with my mom as often as possible or she will flip out. I just hope this thing will work."

"What is flip out?" asked Duddly.

"Go crazy and do things which make no sense," Sam quickly responded.

"I think your *phone* will be just fine," Otly quickly said.

They drove to the edge of town and found a small clearing where Ryan usually parked to go running on forest trails. All four of them got out of the car and Otly sprinkled the top of the car with a pinch of the dust. In a small puff of sparkling dust, the vehicle seemed to disappear.

"You might want to hide it or it will get stepped on," Sam smiled. Ryan picked up his car which was now barely bigger than a match box car. He turned it around in his hand and smiled. "This would really come in handy when there are no parking places at school or the mall. Shrink it and put it in my backpack." He giggled when he pictured how easy that would be. He sat the car near the back of a rock, it would be impossible for anyone else to see it there.

"Time for the two of you." Otly directed. Ryan and Sam stood next to each other as Otly lightly dusted their heads. Once again they both felt that strange tingle in the pit of their stomachs and before they knew it, they were no taller than a couple of inches. Otly asked them both to sit on the Sirasol leaf but Ryan stopped. He pulled out his phone and held it up for Sam to see.

"Sam lets try this real quick, let's see if it works." She dialed, "I will just do our first check in then," she gestured at Ryan. She heard the dial tone and then her mothers voicemail, for a second she was surprised that her Mom didn't answer, but only for a second '*Amazing*', she thought, "Hey mom its me, just doing our first check in and all is great. It's fantastic out here, we should come up later in the year more often." She was truly surprised that the phone still worked after being shrunk to doll house accessory size.

"We really need to get going, I don't mean to rush, but the meeting will start soon and I am not sure if Maliek wanted to speak with you before everything starts." Otly urged them on. They pulled the Sirasol leaf a little further than usual since both of the kids had to sit on it and there was, after all, just the two of them to carry them back to the tree.

Otly and Duddly took off a little slower than usual as they didn't want to drop either of the kids. Ryan started singing "...*off we go, into the wild blue yonder...lalala...lalalala*" Sam smiled, she didn't feel quite as easy about this flying on a leave stuff as Ryan. In less than twenty minutes they were at their destination. The teens were snuck into Maliek's chambers.

"How splendid to see the both of you again, I take it you both had a safe journey?" Maliek smiled. Both of them nodded and smiled in return. Even though they no longer felt intimidated by him, just knowing how old he was still amazed Sam.

"Thank you for thinking of us sir," Sam bowed her head to Maliek, "we both feel honored to be a part of all of this. I noticed there are a lot more Pixies now then there were a few days ago."

"You are right Sam," agreed Maliek, "it was just a day or so after you were last here that the truth was revealed to me how many of my kind had been seen by humans. We also found out that a lot of the stories told to us by the elders were, in fact, untrue. I felt since Faith and Frizzle are now members of the Council they should know the truth."

"Is that why you had us come here?" Ryan asked.

"Oh no, my dear boy," Maliek padded Ryan on the shoulder. "I had you come because you are the first humans visiting the Windhill Tree community, though apparently many of us have met humans, other than you and Sam no one has been inside before. He scratched his beard and added, "all except Mariskina, apparently she's had encounters before." Sam wanted to say something else, but Maliek stopped her, "We shall have time to talk a bit later. I took the liberty of having Ariana and Phinneaus each bring me one of their special outfits. I assumed you wouldn't be dressed for the occasion." The teens looked down at their school clothes and blushed. Maliek hurried to reassure them. "Not that what you are wearing isn't nice," he said with a smile. He handed each of the kids a beautiful outfit. "You might just feel more comfortable in these."

Ryan was to wear an emerald green suit along with a white shirt and matching emerald green tie. Maliek had figured that was more fitting the human style. Sam was given a lavender colored gown, it was wonderful, since it also smelled of lavender. While the kids were changing, Maliek continued with his explanation of what was going on and why they had felt it necessary to hold the meeting. Just as they were to head out the small door a trumpet blew in the crown of the tree. It startled Sam, "Is everything ok?" Maliek patted her arm, "Oh yes my dear it is merely letting us know that it is time to assemble. Sam was about to step out to the little balcony in front of Maliek's door when he pulled her back. "I don't want Faith and Frizzle to see you. You being here is a surprise for them. We shall wait just a moment and let the Council assemble before we go in," Maliek was proud of himself and his surprise. Mariskina and her sister had their news, but he was sure his would be a hit as well.

❧

The double doors to the great hall opened and its entire splendor was revealed. The

room glistened in gold and amber. Red, green, and light brown reflected on each table and the room smelled of cinnamon and nutmeg. It was breathtaking even for the Pixies who had been in the room countless times. It was the first time the room had been decorated to reflect the current season, it was customary to always have spring in the hall. The furnishings in the room had been changed slightly, the usual round table had been replaced with an oval one. In front of the table, rows of chairs had been placed to accommodate as many guests as possible. Mariskina, Maliek, Faith and Frizzle, as well as the rest of the High Council, expected the population in the tree to double for the duration of the meeting. Not only were the invited guests arriving, but most of them had brought family along. Accommodating everyone seemed as hard as keeping track of one's sproutlings. There seemed to be Pixies everywhere, but everyone was happy and accommodating.

The High Council took their seats, it was hard for Maliek not to take his usual seat at the center of the table, but that now belonged to Faith. Everyone was in awe over how much the room had changed and they all agreed that they should continue decorating the hall with current season might be at any special event.

"I need the Council to come to order as quickly as possible, we have an urgent matter to discuss before we begin the meeting." Faith calmly spoke her request as head of Council and she knew her dad would be proud.

"We have been made aware of a situation with Chichine, it appears she wishes to do us harm. She has bewitched the out of boundary birds and has them under her command. She is under the impression that Abby and Polly are under her spell and she has ordered them to have the tree spiders spin a net large enough to trap every one of us and our guests in the tree for the birds to do with as they wish. Frizzle and I believe…"

Oscar interrupted her, "I do not wish to voice disrespect, but do you not find it odd that this occurred only within days after you took over command of the council?"

"I assure you, Oscar, that this planned attack has nothing to do with my position." Faith defended herself.

"Faith, may I make a comment?" Mariskina asked politely.

"Of course, please feel free," Faith gave the floor to Mariskina.

"There are things about Faith that she herself has not become aware of but which are well known to Chichine, myself and her father. We cannot reveal what these things are but be aware that Maliek could not have made a wiser choice than Faith as his replacement. So, Oscar, you are right to a point, but these events were predicted and must take place for our tree to survive." Faith sat in her seat looking as shocked as she could be and Oscar as well as the other council members stared at her. Mariskina squeezed her hand and assured her she had nothing to worry about. Faith new that the old wise one would never say something like that if it were not true so she relaxed – a little.

"Well that's just great," spouted Frizzle, "like I don't have enough to protect her from now there is something else." He laughed out loud and that snapped everyone out of their shocked state.

"Back to matters at hand please," Faith rose and called everyone to attention.

They discussed briefly how to handle the mess with Chichine and Barask came up with a plan as quickly as he usually does. However, they had never faced a situation such as this and were hopeful that Barask and his team could make the necessary preparations. They all felt it was of the utmost importance that neither Chichine or their guests became aware of what had been revealed to the council. Barask left the meeting early as he needed to discuss and plan with his entire team. The remaining Council felt sure they would have nothing to worry about. They knew that though Barask would have loved to attend the presentation of the special guests, their safety as well as everyone else's in the tree was of higher importance for the time being.

"Barask, my brother and I appreciate your sense of urgency and we would love to give you the opportunity to visit with the guests in my chambers once the situation is under control," Faith offered the security chief. He accepted with gratitude and a huge grin. Faith had jumped into her new position with both feet and landed firmly on the ground.

Even though everyone on the High Council seemed to have respect for Chichine, none of them were surprised that things with her had come to this since she had isolated herself more and more from the community. Still, they wondered if anyone would be pleased with the outcome of this dispute, win or lose.

⇒ 16 ⇐
The Introduction of the Guests

After discussing the matters at hand, the council decided it was time to bring in the guests. Maliek informed Mariskina that he also has someone special and they needed to decide who they would bring in first. He felt it may be better if they somehow could add two more chairs to the table.

"Two more?" asked Mariskina suspiciously, "What are you up to?"

He didn't answer but gave her a huge grin and winked.

"Faith…Frizzle…the guests I invited are more or less just for you. I know that especially you Faith have become even fonder of the humans than before, so without further ado…" He got up and walked to the door. Even before he opened the door Faith and Frizzle knew who their father was talking about. Faith jumped out of her seat so fast that it knocked over a chair as she sprinted to the door.

"Yellow speckled stink bug, Dad! I can't believe you did this for us!" She squealed.

The doors opened and Sam and Ryan entered, they both looked beautiful and more like Pixies without wings than humans. Other than Sam not having wings, she and Faith looked almost identical, except Sam still had her freckles. There were hugs and tears and laughter before everyone settled down. The chairs had been re-arranged so Sam and Ryan could sit next to Faith and Frizzle. Holding onto Sam's hand, Faith turned towards her father, "How did you manage to get them here dad?" Maliek felt proud to have given his daughter such a surprise.

"Barask and I actually worked this out together. We sent Otly and Duddly to get them. It wasn't easy since we don't know the rules of the human world. But they managed to get the permission from their elders…" Maliek announced.

"Sir, they are called parents not elders," Ryan interrupted Maliek, blushing when everyone looked at him at once. Maliek just thanked Ryan for the correction and asked if he could explain a little about how they managed to get here.

"It was really interesting, "Ryan began, "Otly and Duddly found me in the parking lot at our school and…" He hadn't counted on the strange looks and questions he got before he finished his first sentence. They asked him to explain what a parking lot, a car, and a school was.

"This should be interesting," Sam smiled at Faith, "he will either have to stop and explain a lot or work around some things with easier words the Council can understand." She was right and by the time Ryan got to the part how his car shrank, everyone understood enough to laugh at the thought of him holding his miniature car.

"I have to say I was very surprised that our mobile phones still worked after being shrunk," he pulled his phone out of his pocket and held it up for all to see, "Sam has already called her mom a few times as she promised she would. After all, we couldn't tell her where we were going." Several of the council members asked if they could take a look at the funny looking contraption. None of them had ever seen anything like it before.

"You are sneaky, aren't you?" Mariskina smiled at Maliek, "what a wonderful surprise and not at all a bad idea for the general purpose of our meeting."

All together satisfied with himself, Maliek sat back and folded his hands over his round belly. They shared a few more stories about Sam and Ryan's trip to the tree and then Mariskina decided they needed to move on.

"Now it's my turn," Mariskina rose and slowly walked to the double door. Some of the council members had started to rise, "you may want to stay in your seats because if these guests have the same effect on you they had on me, you will sit right back down and I wouldn't want you to miss your seat." She had to snicker at her own comment. Those who had gotten up quickly sat back down and shrugged their shoulders.It was after all Mariskina, so why not?

Once again the double doors opened, and Helene entered. Behind her two Pixies followed, covered in hooded capes which hid their faces. Helene floated to the front of the long table and the two mystery creatures followed behind her one on each side.

"What I am about to show you might shatter every belief about our kind you have ever had. There have never been two of us who looked exactly alike. I would have to say Faith and her human friend may be as close as it gets, but they are not of the same race," Helene explained, "before I reveal these two young ladies I would like to tell you a little about how they came to be with us." A chair was brought for her to sit, at her age standing and floating wasn't something she wanted to do for long periods of time.

"We have kept these two hidden for 150 suncycles and you will soon see why we felt it necessary to do so. Their names are Emmi and Saralin, their father's name was

Alexandri. I knew him from Spring Blossom Tree where he met their mother Natalie. She was a beautiful and very bright creature, but we sadly lost her not long after Emmi and Saralin arrived. She became very ill and in the hopes of bringing her back to health with lots of rest, Alexandri took her away. She perished shortly after that and so did their father. You may think there is nothing special about that, things like that happened all the time in the days gone by…but…there was something very special and unusual about their mother," Helene motioned the girls to remove their capes. Awe, amazement, and even some fear spread across the room like wildfire. The only ones not affected by the sight of the twins were Sam and Ryan.

"That's cool," Ryan stated, "Pixie twins."

"Please everyone," Faith motioned for everyone to return to their seats, "let her continue." Turning to Ryan she said, "Would you mind grabbing those two chairs over by the wall so they can sit down as well." Ryan nodded and did as he was asked. He placed a chair behind each of the girls and noticed the amazing color of their eyes. The girls sat down and thanked Ryan.

"Natalie was not her given name," Mariskina continued. "When I first met her she was named Christine. She was not born of a Pixie, but of a human." Helene waited a moment for the latest news to be digested. She continued to tell the Council the story she had told Mariskina earlier that morning. Apprehension and twinges of fear seemed to spread in the room and when she was finished, she told Faith that the girls as well as she were prepared to answer questions.

"I appreciate that you prepared for that," complimented Faith, "If you don't mind, I have a couple of question for the girls."

"Please go ahead Faith," replied Helene.

"Girls," Faith addressed the twins, "Have you ever felt you wanted to explore the human world or better said, have you felt any kind of connection to the humans?"

Emmi rose to answer the question, "I can't say we have. We have never known a life other than that in our tree. Neither of us had ever met our parents and we had been told at a young age that they had loved us very much, but had sadly vanished during a trip. It wasn't until this morning that we heard the details about our mother. We haven't really had time to think about our history, but we are sure Auntie Helene will help us bridge that gap just as she has done with so many other things." She sat back down and Faith thanked her.

"Anyone else?" Helene inquired.

Council member Penelope rose, "First of all, Faith, I would like to say that decorating the great hall to represent the outside was a fantastic idea."

"Thank you, do you have a question for our guests?" said Faith.

"Yes," she faced them, "I'm not sure if this is something that the two of you can answer or if this is something Helene will have to address… why is it that you are identical except for your eyes?" The girls looked at each other and shrugged their shoulders. Helene smiled, "Yes, I will have to take this one. The girls both had blue eyes, but we constantly had trouble telling them apart so we figure out which of them liked green and we gave her green eyes. We made the change just before their mother and father had to leave and it brought them some joy in their sad time."

"How did you manage to change them?" Penelope asked.

"I'm not sure," confessed Helene. "Leofus took care of that as well as a great deal of their education. Changing any physical aspect is something we do only when it is truly necessary. I have learned that in the human world making physical changes is sadly used to define beauty. I don't understand why only few of them believe that their beauty comes from the inside," she paused and seemed to drift off into nowhere as she finished her thought, "why is it so hard for these beings to realize their true beauty?"

"I know I'm not a part of this Council," Sam rose, "but I am curious about something, if it's ok to ask?"

"Why of course," said Helene, snapping back to the moment, "we would love to hear your question."

"Has anything like that ever been done again, I mean, between Pixies and humans, since then?" She asked without hesitation.

"No Miss Sam," Helene seemed to have sadness in her voice when she answered. "The few people who were involved in the *adoption* of Natalie promised that we would never do any such thing again. Not that we didn't want to or didn't have the opportunity to, it is just against nature and our beliefs.

"We have often blamed ourselves that their mother vanished at such a young age because of what we did. Nature has created each being and we, in a large sense, violated that."

"I understand. I really do." Sam quietly sat back down.

"May I ask who all was involved in the change of their mother?" Maliek wanted to know.

"This is the question I was waiting for from either you or Mariskina," Helene smiled, "there was myself, Chichine, Leofus, Beene, Renee, Lena, and two others. Let me think for a moment... Rowina...and...oh one from England...I believe her name was Lizzy."

"Have you kept in touch?" Maliek asked.

"With some of them," Helene responded. "Most of us know Leofus, we couldn't really imagine educating some of our younglings without him could we?" Several of the older council members laughed as they had been taught by Leofus and knew how silly he could be. Yet they would not have traded him for any other teacher.

"Well I don't need to say anything about Chichine other than that I hope Barask and his team are coming along well. Rowina,

Lizzy, and Lena I have not heard from in countless sun cycles. Beene I believe is here for the meeting and currently entertaining some younglings in the tree's main kitchen, which leaves Renee. I had gotten word one of her family members had fallen very ill so she was not able to attend, we do, however, talk on occasion via Batbug."

"If there are no other questions, I would like to move on to the next part of our meeting and invite the general population in, or as many as we can fit," Faith stood up as she spoke. "We could have all of those who have had encounters come in and we can make all the announcements via dust."

"Good idea," said Frizzle.

"Just one more thing," said Helene, "I know the girls haven't had contact with humans, but since their mother was human I thought their existence may show everyone that not only can we live in harmony, we can also do more to help each other."

"Helene?" Sam approached her, "Have you ever heard of Dr. Holley?" Helene took her hands and smiled.

"Yes, yes I have. As a matter of fact I met with him just recently to bring him more herbs and I believe Mariskina knew his great-great-something-grandfather."

"Oh my gosh! I knew it! That is so fantastic. I have to tell Ryan."

"We can talk about it a bit later on if you two would like," stated Helene, "it may help you better deal with your secret."

"That would be lovely, thank you so much." Sam headed off to tell Ryan the news.

"Are you serious?" Ryan was shocked, "I bet that green stuff he had you drink was something the Pixies made for him." Sam nodded in agreement.

Faith declared the Council meeting officially over and hoped that all of them would enjoy the stories they were about to hear as much as she knew she would. It seemed that most of them were taking on a different opinion about those whom they had been afraid of for so long. The Council members spent a few moments in light conversation with the twins as well as the human friends of the Windhill Tree community. Frizzle and Maliek had left to gather the guest speakers who would tell their stories of encounters with humans. Both of them hoped they would be as pleasant as theirs.

⇒ 17 ⇐
Humans Aren't So Bad

Faith, Frizzle, and Maliek went out to the balcony to estimate how many guests and community members wanted to present stories and listen as well.

"There is no way we can make them all fit," proclaimed Frizzle after just a few seconds.

'*You can say that again,*' thought Faith.

"No worries," Maliek scratched his head as if he doubted himself. "We will line up chairs and a podium on the balcony and use dust so we can be heard throughout the tree."

"All that work," Faith sounded sad, "we wanted everyone in the tree to see what we did." She thought for a moment, "Hey, I know! We could have the food lined up in here and then have a line go through. I'm sure those in the kitchen would find it much easier to set everything up here anyway. What do you guys think?"

"That sounds like a great idea," came from Maliek and Frizzle at the same time.

"Dad, can you have the chairs set up along the balcony? Frizzle, you get a podium and inform the rest of the Council about the change. I am going to zip down to the kitchen and let them know we will be setting up in here." She was so excited that everyone in the tree would see what they had done in the hall.

Frizzle flew through the inside of the tree and thinly spread light blue dust, this way he would be able to simply talk and everyone could hear him.

"Friends…may I have your attention please?" Frizzle stood on the balcony with both hands leaning on the railing, "We are thrilled so many of you could join us, however that presented the problem that not everyone will fit into the great hall. We are making some adjustments and will be tending to you momentarily. Would all those who have come to share their story please join the council in the great hall for a moment?"

With a small buzz several of the guests made their way up to the crown of the tree, everyone else assembled in such a manner that they all looked like they were in an auditorium. It was a sight to see. Sam and Ryan had made their way out to the balcony and watched the commotion.

"Can you believe this? I thought last time was amazing, and well it was, but this is just as good if not better." Sam had Ryan by the arm and seemed to be bubbling over with excitement. She even bounced a little just to release some of the energy she felt. Neither of them had much interest in finding out what was going on in the great hall. They would wait and listen to the stories as everyone else. There could not possibly be anything more amazing than Emmi and Saralin. Sam began to wonder if Helene was right about her assumption that Natalie had vanished at such a young age. She had never had an issue with her physical appearance, but she knew many of her friends and girls at school did. She hoped with all her heart that she could continue and even learn more to teach others that the way they looked was just fine.

There just are no logical blueprints for the perfect human being. Her mind wandered to how some of the girls treated each other because of their physical appearance with total disregard to how much their words could hurt. She thought about how much she had disliked Ryan and how much he had ridiculed her because of her beliefs and now he was the one she shared this fantastic secret with.

She shook her head with the thought that unless you give yourself the chance to listen to the thoughts of someone else, you may never know what makes them tick and worse yet, you may lose out on a great friend.

"Share your thoughts," Ryan wanted to know.

"Oh, I was just thinking about some of the girls at school. Those with curly hair want it straight and those with straight hair want it curly. There is constant self-degrading of being too heavy, not tall enough, not this or that enough. There are so many similarities between us and the Pixies, yet that is one thing they don't even think about. Remember when Faith told us that she had been so worried when she started getting freckles?"

Ryan barely got a chance to nod his head much less respond.

"Her biggest concern was that the freckles were a punishment of nature for something she had done. Now she understands that they are a sign that she has a deeper connection to nature and the freckles are a sign for everyone to see. Now imagine those who had helped her learn that difference hadn't been there. Where would she be today?"

"So you think that same principle applies to us?" Ryan wanted to know.

"Yes I do." Sam replied.

"But you never gave up when we were all taunting you about your belief in Pixies. You held on with every fiber of your being and now you have proven all of us wrong. Not that we can talk about it, but I know and I am sorry to say that I was one of the worst." Ryan lowered his head. Now and then he still felt some shame having given her so much grief about her believes.

"Ryan that's not the point, *those beliefs* were nothing physical. What I'm talking about are all the physical things most girls find wrong with themselves. I think if we could think of something to do that would show those girls that they are just fine the way they are, no matter what, then we could make a huge difference." Sam glowed with the thought of bringing something to her friends at school which they may not have given a chance before.

"I think we should check into starting a group, you know some type of support group, in which girls can learn that their inner attributes are what brings out their beauty, not the other way around."

"Hmmmm... that sounds like a great idea," Ryan had now also set the wheels in motion to come up with ideas to make this happen. "We could ask Ms. Spilman to help us, she has done a lot of work like that and I bet she could help us set it up."

"Right, great idea," Sam had a smile from ear to ear, "I think we should include Dr. Holley as well." They hugged and both seemed to be bubbling over with joy.

All the chairs had been set up and the general audience gathered in the hollow of the tree. It was a very interesting sight, all of the Pixies were floating, but it looked as if they were sitting in a half circle, very much like an outdoor auditorium. Faith had thought quickly and while everyone else was busy arranging chairs and setting the great hall up for a banquet style meal she had spread dust along the balcony and duplicated the fall themed decorations. Garlands of red, orange, gold, and deep green draped off the balcony. The inside of the hollow had a warm glow to it, which Frizzle had created. The entire inside of the hollow looked magical, its light, sparkling mist filled the hollow, which gave an appearance of very light fog. The mist had a mild lavender scent to it. It had been used by the Pixies for centuries to calm themselves in stressful situations. It was especially useful to all of the Windhill Tree residents as most of them knew what Chichine was planning.

"Friends, we would like to welcome all of you for this special occasion." Faith addressed the large group. "Never before has there been such a need for all of us to come together and plan our future. Through time, some of us have encountered humans and I am glad to say that it has been wonderful to hear that there has never been an incident during which one of us was purposely harmed. Throughout time, it has been proven again and again that we have been greeted with apprehension but curiosity. From all the stories I have heard, it is apparent that here and there we have done a lot of good with the humans. I strongly feel they have learned a lot from us and if we can continue our outreach to them and teach them positive things, we can help them makechanges. I would like to introduce two humans who have made it possible for my community to see the need for change." She paused and motioned for Sam and Ryan to join her. Sam blushed, she had never been introduced to so many at one time.

"This is Samantha and Ryan," both of the kids waved to the crowd and much to their surprise a lot of them waved back.

"I met these two a short time ago and I am glad to say that having them here has brought about a change of heart in a lot of those in this community. Would any of you like to ask them questions?" Faith paused and scanned the crowd.

"DaNisha go ahead," Faith addressed one of the Pixies in the crowd. She rose above the others. "How do you think your community would react if you told them that there is a Pixie community close to their village?" DaNisha had brought up something Sam had been dealing with for years. She looked at Ryan who again showed traces of shame on his face. Sam stepped closer to the balcony to speak. "The first time I saw a Pixie was years ago on my fifth birthday. Ever since then I have known that your kind is not only real, but you had to be close by. Even though many others told me that, especially when I got older, I should stop believing in such unrealistic things, some part of me just held on to my beliefs. My heart told me otherwise." She smiled and gave the floor to Ryan.

"I gave Samantha a lot of grief over her beliefs and encouraged others to make fun of her. Overall, I believe that is how the general population would greet such information. Most humans find it hard to believe in things they can't really see. I can honestly say the human race is so disconnected from nature and its beauty that we approach it with sarcasm and make excuses not to accept it. As you all well know we are more interested in destroying it for the sake of financial gain than preserving it. I think approaching our town with such information would have to be handled with extreme care and caution."

A murmur of uneasiness went through the crowd.

"It sounds to me as if you have learned a great lesson on how to treat the beliefs of those whom you interact with," DaNisha commented.

"Yes he has," Sam jumped in. "Since we met Faith, he has changed a lot. We really never got along before we met Faith, so it seems odd to those whom we go to school with that we are now best friends. They think there is more to it, none of them know the great secret we share. Only a few have noticed that he has become a lot more accepting of others than he used to be."

"Can you give an example?" DaNisha asked.

"There is a young girl who is bound to a wheelchair and Ryan has been helping her a lot by opening doors for her and has even spent time with her at lunch here and there. He found out that they share a great interest in drawing dragons."

"What is a wheelchair?" Maliek wanted to know. Sam explained it and the crowd grew very silent. It was inconceivable to them that a being couldn't walk for some reason.

Dr. Holley, who had been standing in the background, came forward. Sam's mouth dropped open in shock. How did Dr. Holley get here? Mariskina just smiled and winked at her. Faith introduced him to the community before he spoke.

"My daughter Rachel is a friend of these two and she said that this particular young girl has made a lot of new friends since Ryan has taken an interest in her. That is something that is nice about our kind. Sometimes all it takes is one small action by one person to start a chain reaction."

"Can chain reactions like that be re-created with others?" DaNisha really liked what she was hearing.

"I believe so, it is simply a matter of having a lot of passion for something the way Samantha does and then making it happen." Dr. Holley stated, "I think these two have it in them to bring about huge changes in those of our town." DaNisha thanked them all and expressed her great honor to have met them and she stated that she now felt better about bringing about changes in her community.

"Dr. Holley," Sam grabbed his arm as he stepped away from the balcony. "What are you doing here?" The doctor smiled at her, "I had gotten the Batbug message from Mariskina several days ago to attend, remember all those odd old things in my office?"

"Yeah?" she looked puzzled.

"They came from here. One of my way back relatives was given herbs to heal his father from Mariskina when she was just a young sproutling."

"Shut up!" Sam exclaimed. Dr. Holley cautioned her to listen and they could speak about this more later.

"We would now like to hear from some of those who have had encounters with humans. I would like to introduce Jostin, he comes to us from a tree community close by and has an interesting story." Faith motioned for Jostin to join her and stepped back.

"Greetings friends," he waved at the crowd, which was followed by shouts of well wishes and applause. "It was five suncycles ago that I encountered a human. As you all know, there is an area close to here with a beautiful, what the humans call, Ranch. They keep cattle there and tend the land. Over time it has come to the point that they have had to close it off and not allow the general community to visit. Parts of this wonderful area have already been destroyed by one of the owners by building houses and other things. I was out harvesting wild honey one night when I came across a man who was hunting wild pigs. They do a lot of damage to the land and some of the other animals. He had followed one of them when he found himself trapped, within minutes there was not just one wild pig but several and they had the man surrounded. It was obvious they were looking at him the same as they did some of the other animals they encountered in the forest. I sat on a branch and watched to see what he would do. As the pigs went closer and closer, I could see the panic rising up inside of him. I had to do something, I couldn't just stand there and let him be eaten. I knew the pigs were paying attention to nothing but the man and so I made my approach from behind them, I dusted each of the pigs' tails with a bit of dust and they could no longer move. The man had not seen me and was stunned by the pigs' inability to move. He slowly began to make his way off to one side, still not sure if this odd affect would last awhile or only a brief moment. When he cleared the attack path of the pigs, I flew right up in front of his face. I almost felt bad..." His story was interrupted by a loud swoosh sound and just seconds later the light coming in through the tree's canopy seemed to darken.

Faith, Frizzle, and some of the other Council members looked at each other. They knew this could only mean that the net had been dropped. It had happened much sooner than they had expected.

"We need to move now," Frizzle was determined to not let this get too far. "If we alert everyone here we will have a massive panic on our hands and everyone wanting to get out of the tree." Frizzle told the few Pixies standing near him. "What should we do? We can't...wait, we can spread some dust, which will make the majority of the population oblivious to what is happening." Maliek turned to Mariskina, "do you still have some of that?" She nodded and left to collect the dust. Jostin looked from Faith to Frizzle and back, he understood within seconds that he should just continue his story as to not frighten the listeners. While Faith and the others constructed an emergency plan, Jostin had everyone else laughing.

⇒ 18 ⇐
The Attack

"We have to let everyone know it's not safe in the tree or at least get them in the trunk." Mariskina insisted when she landed next to Maliek with the dust. "We can't possibly imagine how many we will lose if even one of those birds gets inside." She held onto the bag with the dust so hard her knuckles began to turn white.No sooner had she spoken when the screams began.

She and Maliek spun around and were both shocked to see one of the large birds within the tree. It was snapping left and right trying to catch the little delicious morsels.

"STOP!" A voice commanded from above. The bird found itself a place to sit and stopped snapping at the scared and helpless Pixies. Moments later Chichine appeared through the opening in the crown of the tree. Faith, Sam, and Ryan stood near the balcony where only moments earlier Jostin had shared his story. Frizzle joined Maliek and Mariskina, all the others seemed to just want to hide in the shadows or get out of the tree to increase their chances of getting away.

"I want Faith," Chichine announced, "I know she is here and she can present herself to me and spare everyone else or one of you can turn her over to me and your life will be spared..."

"I'm right here Chichine," Faith had flown out into the hollow of the tree without anyone noticing. "There is no reason for you to harm anyone, no one here has hurt you." She seemed very sure of herself and not at all afraid of the old Pixie. Chichine waved her right arm and the resting bird swooped up and grabbed Faith by the back of the neck. It happened so fast that no one had a chance to stop it, yet Frizzle, Otly, Tutle, and several other guards surrounded the birds head. He had said several times since his attack that he wanted nothing more than to get rid of these birds. He remembered all too well what one of them had done to him just days before.

"Do not touch her or the bird," Chichine instructed, "if any of you come near the bird it will snap her neck without a thought." She gave the bird another signal and it flew out of the opening at the top of the tree, Chichine right behind it.

For a split second no one seemed to move and then the tears, chatter, and panic started. The net was still in place over the tree and the only way anyone could get out was through the opening through which Chichine had just left.

Maliek made his way to the podium and shouted, "ORDER, ORDER........PLEASE EVERYONE SETTLE DOWN!" The crowd grew quiet enough for him to speak. "We will do our best to get all of you out safely but we can only do this in an orderly fashion. If you all try to get out at once we will have several injuries and we don't want that, as I am sure neither do you.

While Maliek attempted to calm the crowd Jostin, Frizzle, Tutle and Phinneaus made their way out though the opening in the bottom of the tree near the entrance to the security offices. Ryan had wished nothing more than to be able to go with them but Barask assured him that he would be of great help organizing things in the security rooms. Sam stayed with Mariskina and it took all the old one had in her to calm the young girl. Mariskina knew instinctively that Sam had never been so scared in all of her life.

The boys got outside just in time to see which tree Chichine disappeared into but before they could follow, the other birds were closing in and they had to retreat. Without a way to follow Chichine, they made their way to the security offices. Maliek, in the meantime, seemed to have all the guests under control. Many of the residents, those who weren't afraid they might get eaten, helped Maliek try to get everyone out safely. Chichine had who she wanted so there was no reason for her to go after anyone else. The birds were another story. Whenever someone tried to get out, the birds were right there. There was only one other option, they had to guide everyone out through the opening in the trunk. If only few of them left at a time they would go unnoticed by the birds. Maliek called on Seraphina and Jade to help him divert everyone. Both of them were guests, but had impeccable skills to preserve calm and serenity. Within minutes they had everyone gathered in the hollow of the tree.

"Friends," Maliek called out and the group became silent. "In order to avoid the birds, we will need to get you out through a small opening near the security offices in the trunk of the tree. Even though Chichine promised no harm would come to anyone, it seems she forgot to inform the birds." He smiled, hoping someone would laugh, but he waited in vain. Everyone just stared back at him with looks of terror on their faces. The small group had decided to get the oldest ones out first and then go in alphabetical order. It seemed to be accepted and worked well. Three to four Pixies exited every few minutes. In the meantime, Mariskina had calmed Sam down enough to try and engage her in some activity. She instructed her to make lots and lots of sandwiches. Surely by now, everyone was hungry and they would all appreciate a snack. Sam had told Mariskina that she enjoyed cooking and it seemed only logical now that this would keep Sam busy for some time and would give her time to see what plan they had come up with. Surely every milie wasted, Faith was in more danger. Mariskina called Ariana and Nevah to serve the food Sam, and several others, had prepared to all the guests in the tree and help her in any way they could. With that she left, heading down the trunk. She stopped half way there, hovering in midair, apparently in deep thought. Without looking back, she turned and headed to her home. Her window faced east, away from where she assumed the tree was in which Chichine was holding Faith captive. She landed in front of her door and went inside, heading straight for the window. Without a second thought, she opened the window and squeezed through it. She landed on a branch just outside of her window. The birds were watching the top of Windhill Tree and several of them were hovering around the crown of the tree just to the west. That must be where Chichine had Faith.

She flew down to grass level and crept towards the tree at that low level. She managed to make her way up the trunk and into the crown. She didn't have far to go to find Faith and Chichine. It was obvious that Faith was injured. Mariskina got as close as she could without being seen and settled on a branch.

"...why should I allow you and your brother to ruin what it has taken generations to build?" Chichine growled at Faith. "Frizzle does not have the strong connection to nature, which you seem to possess and your fate is as of yet not fully known but to a few old ones, but it cannot be allowed to come to pass." Mariskina had no idea what the conversation was about but she believed the humans played a part in it.

"I was there when they changed that human child into a Pixie and I knew then what had been done was wrong. I knew it went against thousands of suncycles of nature's traditions. They claimed that they had no knowledge of any problems when Natalie left so ill she couldn't care for her children, but I know better." Chichine went on and on. Faith was visibly in pain.

"What does all of that have to do with me?" she cried.

"You...you brought the humans to the tree!" Chichine shouted.

"You separated yourself from us long before that," Faith insisted, seemingly not concerned about her injuries at the moment. "Ever since I began to change according to natures desires, you have been more and more distant, as if all of that was my fault. It would have suited you just fine had I not returned the day of my ceremony."

"Be silent." Chichine glared at her and nodded at one of the birds. It grabbed Faith's wing and pulled her back breaking the wing. Faith cried out in pain.

"You will mind your words, young one." Chichine instructed. "I can bring your end about much faster if you so desire."

Mariskina could see that Faith's right wing was broken. What on earth and precious nature was keeping Barask and his boys?

The situation at the security office was heated at best. It seemed every one of the team

leaders had their own ideas on how to make this work.

"QUIET!" Ryan screamed. He wasn't really sure yet what he was going to say, but he knew that he was tired of all this arguing and noise. "We need a reasonable plan," he suggested. "I was just thinking," he at that moment had a great idea, "if I could, for the time being, be returned to my normal size, I could scare the birds away or distract them long enough for a team of you to get inside the tree."

Barask thought about that for a moment and agreed, "That is the best idea I have heard so far. It can be done. Otly go find Mariskina and get some of that dust from her."

"We still have some from when we went into town." Otly stated and went to retrieve the bag. Barask and some of the others made their way outside. Standing in the grass they observed the small groups leaving every few minutes. It took Otly what seemed like forever to return with the dust. Ryan was back to his normal size in a flash and headed to the tree. None of them knew Mariskina was gone.

Ryan knew that he would not be able to reach the top of the tree to scare the birds, not without climbing it. He picked up several rocks and started running at the tree making as much noise as he could and throwing the rocks. The birds flew out of the tree but not too far away. There was enough space for Otly's team to get into the crown without the birds noticing. Ryan saw them coming and continued to pick up rocks to toss and yelling at the top of his lungs.

Meanwhile, in the great hall Sam was wondering what all the noise was about and she sent Seraphina out to look.

"Your friend is out there throwing rocks at a tree and yelling at it." She told Sam upon her return. Sam felt and looked as puzzled as the little Pixie, but knew she had no time to go find out what was going on. She was sure it was all in an attempt to get Faith back. The knot in her stomach got tighter every time she thought about her friend.

Otly and several of his team members had made it safely to the inside of the tree. He had to smile at Ryan's one-of-a-kind strategy. Slowly, the team made its way closer and closer to Faith and Chichine. They could hear the two of them debating.

"Holy bat wings," Otly stammered. "What is Mariskina doing here?"

The whole team came to a halt and they all looked into the direction of Otly. He pointed and they all saw the old wise one on a branch not too far away. One minute she was peacefully sitting on a branch and the next she was floating towards Chichine.

"I've hear about enough out of you," Mariskina stated as she flew between Faith and Chichine, "Faith had nothing to do with Natalie or with her changes. You're just an angry old bat who fights progress with all you can...well not anymore." Mariskina was fully aware at the risk she was taking and she knew that the next for moments would be her last. She knew there was no other way she could save Faith. It was only moments until Faith's light would begin to dim and she would fall into the purple hue. No sooner had she had that thought she could feel the bird's beak stabbing her back, the tip of it exiting through her mid-section. She managed to turn to Faith.

"Live well, young one. My love will always be with you." There was a puff of purple hue and she was gone.

"NOOOOOOOOOOOO..." Faith screamed and the tears began to flow.

"You better cooperate or you will meet the same fate." Chichine warned her. Otly and his team sat as if petrified for seconds before Otly instructed Tutle to head back to the tree along the grass line and get more help.

"What are you doing back here?" Barask wanted to know.

"She's killed her…she killed Mariskina," Tutle could barely keep his voice steady. Everyone in the office heard what he said and the room became instantly silent. Barask sent one of the others to go collect Maliek but to not reveal why he was needed. They returned moments later along with Leofus. Barask shared the tragic news and Leofus began to weep silently.

"Sir, I don't mean to be disrespectful, but we do still have Faith to worry about." Tuttle gently suggested.

"The boy is right," Leofus sniffled, "we need to act now and if you all don't mind, I'd like to come along to the other tree. She turned this into something it didn't need to be." He tapped himself on his head with his wand and turned into a Batbug, which Tutle could easily carry.

"You two please be careful," Barask instructed. "We don't need to lose anyone else." Within moments Tutle and Leofus were back in the other tree and Leofus had turned back into a Pixie-size wizard. Faith's condition had worsened, she had blood running from her arms and head and her other wing was broken as well. The bird had pecked at her head several times.

"I am going to make your death as painful as you have made my life." Chichine was only inches away from Faith. "Knowing what happened to the old one, do you honestly think any of them are brave enough to come for you?" She laughed out loud as she raised Faith's blood streaked face.

"Chichine that will be about enough!" Leofus announced.

All color left Chichine's face as she noticed the tip of his wand pointing straight at her. She signaled the bird, which immediately made a move for the old wizard. Leofus shouted "Reverso obliviouso" and pointed the wand at the bird, which immediately left the tree. Chichine charged at Leofus with a dagger he had given her long ago when she was still part of the tree-family. "Totenall," was the only word he spoke while quickly pointing the wand at her and she was gone in a hue of purple. He knew that had been his only choice to save not only Faith and the others but himself as well, as one scratch with that dagger would have sent him to his death.

"We need to erase the spell from the other birds so we can get Faith back home and to the infirmary." Otly pointed at Faith, a pale purple hue had become visible, she was holding onto life with all she had. Milo took Leofus to the top of the tree where he removed the spell one bird at a time. Ryan was still making noise and running around, so the birds left as fast as they could. Otly sent one of the other guards down to him to let him know he should go back to the tree that everything had been settled and they would shrink him back to Pixie size. Two others collected a Sirasol leaf and they gently laid Faith on it. She was in bad shape and they knew they were running out of time.

Once they had her in the emergency infirmary, Otly went to collect her brother and father to be by her side. Tutle collected Sam who was just sitting on a chair in the kitchens. She was weak and barely able to move, tears silently rolling down her face.

"Is she dead?" she whispered.

"No," Otly knelt in front of Sam. "No, she's not. She badly injured, but she will be fine. I need to take you to see Maliek though, ok?"

She nodded. Sam being much smaller than Otly, he picked her up and flew her down to the infirmary. She hugged Maliek and Frizzle and saw that both of them had been crying, and so had Ryan. All of them realized that Sam had no idea that Mariskina was gone.

"Sam, "Maliek took her hand, "I need to tell you something."

"Faith is all right, Otly said," Sam's hands were shaking, "she's gonna be fine right?"

"Yes...yes of course, my dear," Maliek reassured her, "but I'm sorry, we lost Mariskina." Sam covered her mouth and swallowed hard. Dr. Holley grabbed hold of her just as he came out of the infirmary and sat her down in a nearby chair.

"Good news," he turned his attention to the others. "Faith is fine and resting. We were able to set her wings and mend them. The wounds on her head and arms have been treated and bandaged. She is resting and you can all see her in just a little while."

Everyone present began to hug each other and smile. Ryan knelt by Sam holding her hand. "How can they all be so happy, they lost Mariskina?" Sam asked in slight disbelief.

Maliek heard the question and turned to Sam, "My dear child, she's not gone as you would think. She has just moved on to a different state in nature." He patted her hand, "she would not be happy if she knew we shed more than a few tears for her. It is our tradition to celebrate the life of one who is no longer with us."

Sam smiled and wiped her tears away. They all knew that one part of life had ended, but another was just beginning.

≫ 19 ≪
Natalie and Alexandri

S am and Ryan hugged each other and Dr. Holley had his arms around both of them. It seemed to be the same throughout the tree, some crying, others smiling with relief and some even laughed. Sam lifted her head and saw Frizzle and Maliek not too far from them. Maliek's face was dirty and smeared from the trail of tears. All of them knew Mariskina had not vanished in vain and they all knew a part of her would live on in them all.

Most of the guest had left with the knowledge that the threat to their community was over and that soon they would all celebrate their Harvest Festival together. Only those living at Windhill Tree and the special guests were floating and standing about. It seemed as if no one wanted to go to sleep. They all felt as if they went to sleep, their memories would be less bright in the morning. No one wanted to speak, there was a serene silence in the tree and all that could be heard was the wind mildly brushing the outside of the tree as if to let the community know that all would be well.

"Children," a soft voice came from the balcony in front of the great hall. "I know we are all saddened by the events this afternoon, but all of you as well as I know that she would not have wanted us to grieve for her but to celebrate her life," Helene spoke softly. Sam could see she had spent a good amount of time crying. Her eyes were swollen and red. "I think we should all go to our rooms and rest for the night. Tomorrow we can plan something special to remember those we have lost."

Most of the Pixies bowed their heads as a sign of respect to Helene for her loss. Even though some of them had lost family members as well, they all knew how much Mariskina meant to the community as a whole, as well as across the entire Pixie community throughout the world.

Sam, Ryan, and Doc Holley approached Maliek and Frizzle. "I'd like to go see how Faith is doing," Sam wiped her nose on the back of her hand.

Maliek hugged her. "Of course, we should all go to the infirmary."

Helene joined them and, out of kindness to those who couldn't fly, all of them took the staircase leading down the trunk of the tree.

"She will be fine right?" Sam could not stop the tears from running. Ryan was worried about her, he had never seen Sam this emotional before. Maliek took her hand and squeezed gently. "Yes dear, she will be fine," he tried to smile.

"I wish I had your faith and mental strength," she sniffled and gave a small smile.

"How nice," Maliek was glad to see her smile, "you found something to make you happy. "It's not that," Sam told the old Pixie, "the humans use the word faith a lot, is has to do with belief. I just think we often use that word and don't really pay attention to it."

"Helene?"Emmi called her softly, "can I ask a question?"

"Certainly, my dear." Helene replied taking the young Pixies hand.

"I'd like to know the whole story of our parents." Emmi stated very matter-of -factly.

"I think we can arrange that soon," Helene squeezed her hand. "Let's wait until we get to Faith's bedside, as I'm sure she would like to hear as well." Emmi nodded.

The small group had made their way down the long spiral staircase and had reached the infirmary. Reality hit them when they saw the multitude of injured Pixies. Every single bed in the ward was occupied and so was every chair. Dr. Holley's face darkened, he so wanted to help but knew his medicine wouldn't help in this magical environment.

"At least I can help apply bandages and ointments," he said to himself and pushed passed Sam and Faith. He quickly found one of the Pixies looking after those injured. All of the tree's residents knew him and they put him to work in no time.

"Excuse me," Sam asked one of the attendants, "where might we find Faith?"

"Of course, Sam," the young one smiled, "she's been waiting for you."

The attendant quickly led the small group to a little room in the back of the infirmary. Gently opening the door she peaked inside. The room was scarcely lit as to not keep its occupant from sleeping. "Faith," she announced, "they are all here."

They all piled into the small room and the attendant brightened the lights. Faith looked worse than they had expected and she realized what they were thinking.

"It's over. I'll be fine. She didn't manage to do what she had set out to do." She tried to smile at her visitors. Thinking about her teacher and most trusted friend made it hard for her to hold back the tears.

"Guess what, Faith," Sam tried to cheer her up, "Helene is going to share the whole story of Emmi and Saralin's origins." Faith looked at Helene who nodded and they smiled at each other. A knock on the door startled everyone out of their thoughts. The door opened and one of the attending nurse Pixies asked if the group wanted some tea and biscuits. It was a welcome suggestion.

When she came back with the goodies just minutes later, they had all made themselves as comfortable as possible. Ryan and Frizzle had fetched some more chairs and Sam had checked in with her mom again. Hiding her sadness was the hardest things she'd done in a long time, but there was just no way she could let her mom know what was going on. It helped a lot to let her know that they had run into Dr Holley and they would be staying with him.

"Helene, I think now would be a good time." Saralin suggested to her guardian.

"Yes," Frizzle chimed in, "I think we could all use something to take our minds of the current events." He tried to smile, but it didn't amount to much.

"Well," Helene rearranged herself on her chair, "if you insist. I guess it will have to be done sooner or later and sooner is just as good a time as any."

Saralin and Emmi both sat on the floor on either side of Helene while everyone else made themselves comfortable.

"I know it has been about 150 sun cycles ago," she began. "I had often taken herbs to a human orphanage not far from my home tree. A young girl by the name of Christine had been brought to the orphanage just days before my last visit and the head mistress was always proud to show me their new arrivals." She paused for a moment. "They really did try to treat all of the younglings as if they were part of a large family." Helene stroked Emmi's head.

"The first time I met your mother, she was a sproutling just a few days old. Her mom had passed after complications from birth and no one seemed to be able to locate any other living relatives. Somehow, and to this day I am not sure how this could have been, but this little sproutling could communicate with me. I could hear her thoughts as clear as sunshine. This had never happened with a human of any age. I went to visit her often and the day came on which I spoke with the head mistress about making little Christine one of my family. I told her I would have to consult the High Council to see what we could do as I was sure nothing like I had planned had ever been done."

Helene rose from her chair to refill her small cup with tea. "At first the Council was very reluctant. We had no idea what to make my plan a reality and worse yet, we had no idea would the potential long term side effects might be."

"What did you want to do?" Saralin asked eagerly.

"Patience little one," Helene patted the young Pixie's head and sat back down.

"After much deliberation, we concluded that it would take six of the highest Council members about two caspens to create a dust potent enough to bring little Christine down to our size. On the full moon in the next caspen the High Council members and Leofus met at the orphanage. Christine was separated from the other children and the magic began." Helene took a deep breath and looked around the room. All eyes were on her, human and Pixie alike. "By the way," her attention went to Sam and Ryan, "A caspen is about one month in human time." Everyone laughed a little and even Faith seemed to have forgotten about her pain and appeared bright-eyed and alert. "The head mistress destroyed all of Christine's records." Helene continued, "Since no family had been found for the girl, no one would miss her. It was a long night and we completed a dusting of the little sproutling each hour. At times we thought we would have to stop because she would just seem to be in agony at times. We got through the night and all of us managed a little sleep. I left with the little sproutling just before dawn and after all of them had decided that her new name would be Natalia. Of course, even though she had wings now she couldn't fly yet. We had to teach her. Within a sewens she had adapted so well no one could have ever guessed she wasn't born of Pixie parents. It seemed as if no time had passed and she had grown into a beautiful youngling and she had fallen head over wings in love with a boy named Alexandri. Of course, the two of them were much too young. About your age Faith," she turned and smiled at Faith. Sam and Ryan were smiling at each other and Frizzle watched them, grinning to himself.

"When she was finally able to marry Alexandri, she was 92, which is still young for a Pixie to think about starting a family. I suppose in human years she would have been 18 and that's a bit young to get married right?" Helene turned her attention to Sam.

"There are some who do get married that young, like when my parents were young it was done a lot, but not anymore," Sam informed everyone.

"It seemed that very little time passed and Natalia announced that she was with sproutling. Everyone was excited. We celebrated as the time drew closer for the little one to arrive, even Leofus came for the special occasion. Things didn't go as we expected. Beene had been taking care of the young couple for some time and between her, me and Leofus, we couldn't figure out what was happening. Something occured that none of us could have anticipated nor did we ever think anything like this could happen. She didn't have one sproutling, but two. The one thing we had not considered when we shrunk her was that her human genes would not change. The little ones were healthy as could be, and their little wings developed beautifully. That was one of our biggest concerns. The healthier the two little ones grew, the sicker their mom became. It was as if something had happened to her after the girls were born. She hid her illness for the longest time, even Alexandri didn't know.

"By the time the girls were ten suncycles, Natalia could no longer function on her own. We all took turns caring for her, but she was sad because she could no longer care for her children. Alexandri didn't want to make matters worse for her and he knew that the girls were more than well cared for with Beene and me. The two of them decided to go off into the deep forest and let Mother Nature decide what was to happen. We made no fuss about their departure and all of us hoped with all of our hearts that they would return.

"Three suncycles later, the girls came to live with me full time. Leofus found Alexandri just a little while after Natalia had vanished and there was no talking him into returning to his children. He wanted to remain where his wife had left the world. He asked Leofus to reverse the effects of the lighting ceremony. Leofus reluctantly accommodated him. In time, he would have lost his powers and his wings and shortly after that he would have vanished. No one ever heard from him again.

We just had these two beautiful little Pixies to remember them by." Helene wiped tears from her eyes, "and they couldn't be more perfect."

She kissed each of the girls on the head.

The room was silent. Everyone seemed to have gotten a little teary and no one wanted to speak. The little room had grown dark and one of the nurse Pixies came in to light candles. The sun was setting and Sam and Ryan knew they'd have to be returning home all too soon. Emmi and Saralin remained quiet on the floor holding hands with silent tears running down their faces. It had been the first time in their lives that they had heard the story of their parents. Helene noticed that the twins seemed to be drifting into sadness and solitude.

"Girls," she knelt down next to them despite her age. "You have to know that all of us love you and your parents could not have loved you more. There were things we could never have known before your mother became one of us and if there is one thing I am sure about, I know deep within my heart if she were here today and you could ask her if she had wanted her life to be different she would have said no if it meant not having the two of you." She hugged the girls and kissed each of their cheeks. "Your mom and dad loved each other so much, the two of you were, as Beene would say, the icing on the cake of their beautiful life."

Both the girls smiled and wiped away the tears. They knew Helene was right.

"I hate to be a spoilsport, but Sam and I need to be getting back We told her we wouldn't be more than a few hours," Ryan said after clearing his throat.

"Last time I talked to mom I told her that we had run into Doc Holley but he's ready to go as well." Sam told him.

Faith lowered her head, she didn't want her friend to leave. Sam didn't even feel like a friend, she felt more like a sister. The rest of the guests would be leaving soon and who would she have to confide in? Her beloved Mariskina was gone. Helene sensed Faith's sadness and sat on the small bed next to her.

"Would it please you if Saralin, Emmi, and I stayed here?" She gently asked Faith. Her face lit up. "Would you? Could you?"

Saralin and Emmi smiled at each other, they had briefly overheard Mariskina and Helene discussing the matter, but had no idea what they had decided.

"My sister and I came to the conclusion that it might be better for the girls to continue their lives here with Pixies of their own age. After raising them all these years, life without them wouldn't be right, so I thought I would stay as well. Mariskina's home is big enough…"she paused and a tear came to her eye. "Guess it doesn't need to be big enough for both of us does it?"

Emmi got up and hugged Helene, "It'll be all right Aunt Helene, we have a big family here."

Sam sat next to Helene on Faith's bed. "I'm so sorry". The old one squeezed her hand as if to let her know that everything would be fine."

Maliek cleared his throat. "Otly and Duddly are ready to take you back to your vehicle. Otly has been given authorization to dust you. I am sure you understand that under the circumstances we cannot accompany you."

"I can go with them," Frizzle announced, "I can dust them as well."

"It's settled then, Frizzle will accompany the guards and I will stay with Faith and Helene." Maliek seemed happy with himself.

"Can we go as well?" Emmi wanted to know. Both Maliek and Helene agreed. Saralin opened the door and waited for everyone else to follow. Sam remained seated on the small bed. "May I have a moment alone with Faith?"

"Of course my dear," Helene replied. Ryan hugged Faith, wished her well and told her that he hoped they would see each other again very soon. Faith kissed him on the cheek and smiled at him as he followed the others out the door. The door shut and Sam was alone with Faith. The two of them didn't need many words. Faith tried to lean forward to hug her friend but the broken wing prevented her from moving much. Sam moved closer and hugged Faith instead. The two of them sat there in silence and neither could help the tears from rolling down their cheeks. Minutes seemed to pass and there was a knock on the door. Ryan peaked in "Sam we really need to get going."

"I know, "she said without moving away from Faith, "just one more second."

The door shut.

"Will I see you again soon?" she sniffled.

"I'm sure of it," Faith smiled. Another silent moment passed.

Sam coughed and cleared her throat. The tears were choking her up a bit.

"You know…when us humans believe in something with all of our hearts, we call that faith." She smiled at her friend, "I've just always known that I would someday find mine!"

With that she got up and walked to the door.

Faith smiled, "I know deep down in my heart that we were meant to be sisters." Sam nodded and smiled. She walked out the door to join the others and in less than an hour she and Ryan were back in the car on the way to town with Dr Holley in the back seat.

None of them spoke a word. They didn't need to. They knew that they would have to get back to Windhill Tree for Mariskina's memorial, one way or another. Ryan pulled up in front of Sam's house. She leaned over, kissed him on the cheek and got out of the car. She leaned down on the window and looked at Ryan, he nodded. Sam went into the house and Ryan left to drop off the Doctor and then headed home. They all knew they would be returning to the Pixies very soon.

THE END

Sabine Chennault came to the United States in 1981, and she has been creating stories since her teen years in Germany. Mother to three children and grandmother to four grandchildren, she lives with her husband Lance (Retired Navy Corpsman) and their two Huskies in Washington State. Sabine has a degree in Culinary Arts, English Literature, and Family Counseling.

www.palomabooks.com

Made in the USA
Monee, IL
12 May 2020

30502701R00102